THE POWYS MURDERS

DI GILES BOOK 22

ANNA-MARIE MORGAN

For Jean and Christopher, with love.

ALSO BY ANNA-MARIE MORGAN

In the DI Giles Series:

Book 1 - Death Master

Book 2 - You Will Die

Book 3 - Total Wipeout

Book 4 - Deep Cut

Book 5 - The Pusher

Book 6 - Gone

Book 7 - Bone Dancer

Book 8 - Blood Lost

Book 9 - Angel of Death

Book 10 - Death in the Air

Book 11 - Death in the Mist

Book 12 - Death under Hypnosis

Book 13 - Fatal Turn

Book 14 - The Edinburgh Murders

Book 15 - A Picture of Murder

Book 16 - The Wilderness Murders

Book 17 - The Bunker Murders

Book 18 - The Garthmyl Murders

Book 19 - The Signature

Book 20 - The Incendiary Murders

Book 21 - The Park Murders

Book 22 - The Powys Murders

In the DI McKenzie Series

Book 1 - Murder on Arthur's Seat

Book 2 - Murder at Greyfriars Kirk

Copyright © 2024 by Anna-marie Morgan

All rights reserved.

No part of this book may be reproduced in any form or by any electronic or mechanical means, including information storage and retrieval systems, without written permission from the author, except for the use of brief quotations in a book review.

1

SCARED TO DEATH?

The forest loomed, a monstrous gnarled beast in the darkness. Branches clawed at Ben's face as he crashed through the undergrowth, heart pounding, lungs burning. He couldn't stop. Mustn't stop. His foot caught on a protruding root and he crashed to the ground, pain shooting through his ankle.

He cursed through ragged breaths, forcing himself up, blinking dirt from his eyes, and limping onward through the inky blackness, each step sending agony up his leg. Piercing pain shot through his ribs. Maybe some were broken. He placed a hand on his right side as extra support. That's where it hurt most. He wished he was home, but he couldn't stop running.

In the distance, a twig snapped. He froze, eyes darting around. Was someone there? "Tom?" He held his breath. "Hayden?" His answer was silence and the frantic thud of blood in his ears.

He stumbled on, trying to quiet his footfalls, fear twisting his gut.

As the trees thinned, he found himself in a small clearing. A thin sliver of moonlight filtered down, enabling a dizzying *glimpse of his surroundings. He looked up. Snow was falling again as the moon clouded over. The flakes started small, but quickly grew into large feathers swirling about him. He carried on, vision blurred from pain and the rapidly developing blizzard.*

Ben's injured leg gave out beneath him, and he collapsed to the ground, chest heaving from exhaustion. He lay, shivering from cold and fear as snow stuck to his clothing. "Please... don't let me die like this," he begged the night, seeing his friends in his mind's eye lying lifeless and broken in the darkness.

Tom scrambled up the embankment, *trees looming above, their twisted branches stretching like fingers through the darkness. His thumping heart pounded his ribs as he stumbled over snow-covered roots.*

"Where are you?" he called, in a voice strangled by fear and exertion. The only response was the rustle of snow-covered leaves as his feet travelled through them, and the howling of wind through the trees.

Snow was falling again, swirling around as the wind whipped it up.

Wide-eyed and dizzy, he collapsed onto the frozen earth, breathing ragged and laboured. Dread had taken root, his mind paralysed with terror. He gasped for air, thoughts turning back to earlier that night: the taste of cheap lager on his tongue; laughter echoing off the walls of the pub; the company of friends now lost in darkness.

"Get up," he urged himself, knees cracking under the strain. "Keep moving. Stay here, and you'll die." Muscles shaking, and with hazy vision, he tried rising to his feet. But his shattered, cold-riddled body refused. He felt the butterfly touch of snowflakes on his lashes before his eyes closed for the last time.

. . .

A SHOELESS HAYDEN carried on running, back drenched in sweat. His feet snagged a fallen branch, and he stretched out his hands for protection as he tumbled to the ground. It jarred every bone and joint. Everything hurt. Rising, he set off once more, clawing at his coat and its suffocating fabric. With shaking hands, he tore it free, flinging it to the forest floor, not caring it was the only source of warmth as the temperature continued to plummet. Hypothermia was taking hold. He had long since lost the feeling in his feet. The canvas shoes he wore provided little or no protection against the frigid chill of the Mid-Wales countryside, which had already soaked them through.

"Dammit," he muttered, trying to control each rasping breath so he could listen for his friends. Where were they? "Tom? Ben?" He called, stilling to listen for their return shouts. None was forthcoming. His only answer was the howling wind as wet snow lashed his face. He continued on, forcing one heavy foot in front of the other, blood coursing past his ears as though trying to escape the vessels which bore it. A burning in his lungs accompanied each ice-cold breath. The young man bit his lip, suppressing the urge to call his friends again. He daren't risk it another time. He stumbled on, growing weaker. Each time he fell, it took longer to rise and continue his run into the wilderness.

When his legs finally gave out, Hayden crumpled to the ground, landing amid the snow and tangled undergrowth. He curled into a ball, wrapping his arms around himself, and sobbed. Hot tears mingled with frigid water. All around his fading form, the wind moaned and the snow cover grew.

2

JOY INTERRUPTED

Yvonne took Tasha's hands, gazing into her eyes in the Newtown Registry office in Dolerw Park. It had been a long time coming, but they were now about to make their union official. The DI wore a cream skirt suit; her partner an Italian-made, grey trouser suit.

"I, Tasha, take you, Yvonne, to be my lawfully wedded wife. To love, honour, and cherish, in good times and bad, until death do us part." The psychologist placed a simple gold band on Yvonne's hand and gave it a gentle squeeze.

The DI blinked back tears. "I, Yvonne, take you, Tasha, to be my lawfully wedded wife. To have and to hold, in sickness and in health, for richer or poorer, as long as we both shall live," she recited, trembling as she placed the reciprocal band on her partner's finger.

In the front row, Yvonne's sister sat with her children, Tom and Sally, dabbing at her eyes. After years of watching Yvonne devote herself to police work, Kim felt elated to see her sibling finally commit to the love of her life.

The registrar smiled at the couple. "By the power vested

in me, I pronounce you lawfully wed. You may now kiss the bride."

Tom and Sally grinned as their aunt made her vows. Though still young, they understood the significance of marriage. Sally held on to her mother's arm, as Kim blew her nose into a hanky.

Yvonne's Newtown colleagues and a few of Tasha's friends from the Met cheered and clapped in support.

Eyes glistening, the couple turned to face the congregation. It was time to celebrate.

Whistles and shouts of congratulations accompanied the pair out of the registry office, as the photographer lined up his shots, and the beaming couple shook hands with their loved ones as they filed out.

Dewi clasped the DI's hand. "I'm so happy for you, Yvonne. You deserve this. I wish you all the happiness in the world."

Callum gave her a hug. "Best of luck to you and Tasha. I know you'll be as great a wife as you are a detective," he grinned. "God help your lovely wife, though, if she ever cheats. You will have her pegged before the thought even enters her head."

Dai laughed, giving his colleague a gentle shove. "You can't say things like that on her wedding day." He grabbed Yvonne's and Tasha's hands. "I know you two will be happy together." He flicked his head towards Callum. "And don't listen to him."

The well-wishes continued to flow as everyone took their turn at shaking hands with or hugging the couple.

Yvonne spotted her sister weaving through the crowd, still dabbing her eyes, the children trailing behind, waiting for their turn to hug their aunt.

Kim embraced her, tears streaming down her cheeks. "I'm so proud of you," she whispered, choked with emotion. "Dad would have been so happy to see you settled again."

Yvonne swallowed at the mention of their father. "Thank you, sis. Having you and the children here means everything."

"I'm sorry mum couldn't make it." Kim pulled back. "She wanted to be here, you know."

"I know..." The DI pressed her lips together. "Life gets busy sometimes." She turned her head to hide the disappointment.

Yvonne's nephew and niece caught up. "Auntie Yvonne, you look beautiful," Sally declared, sweeping blond curls from her face as the icy breeze caught them.

"That kiss was gross," added Tom with a grin, eliciting a laugh from his mother and aunt.

The DI grabbed them both, hugging them tight. She had tried always to be there for Kim and the children, and was glad they could share in her joy. It mattered more than anything.

Her face ached from smiling so much in the cool air. Around them the snow, which had lain thick throughout February, melted in fresh March sunshine.

"Come on, you lot, let the brides have centre stage..." DCI Llewelyn gently nudged his colleagues away to avoid them photo bombing the couple until it was their turn to pose.

Yvonne laughed, sparkling blue eyes missing nothing. "It's all right, Chris... I asked the photographer to capture everybody being themselves. Casual images are always the best, don't you think?"

Callum grinned, throwing an arm around her shoulders. "Too right. Now smile..."

Music thumped in the background as they arrived at the Elephant and Castle for the reception. The photographer took the last of his pictures before packing his gear away. Yvonne was glad to get inside. She tucked herself against Tasha, basking in her new wife's warmth. The psychologist planted a kiss on the DI's forehead, thinking she had never looked more beautiful or content.

DCI Everard from the Met called for attention. "Alright, you two, we've got a little something for you." He nodded to DC Singh, who came forward with a gift in silver wrapping.

"Just a little token," Everard explained, shrugging broad shoulders. "Something to put on the mantlepiece." There was a rich warmth to his gruff, cockney voice.

Yvonne unwrapped a framed photo of her team and the psychologist on the job, with a plaque that read: 'Partners in Life and Crime - Congratulations Yvonne & Tasha.'

"It's perfect," she said, holding it up for everyone to see. "Thank you."

Dewi approached with glasses of champagne. "A toast to the happy couple," he called, raising his glass high.

"To Yvonne and Tasha," the congregation said in unison.

The psychologist slipped an arm around her wife's waist. "Thank you all for being here. It means the world to us."

Yvonne nodded. "I can't tell you how much your support has meant to me since moving here. I'm so fortunate to have found not only my soulmate..." She turned to gaze at Tasha, "but also the best friends and colleagues anyone could wish for."

As normal chatter resumed, Tasha leaned in close. "Fancy some air, wife?" she asked.

Yvonne nodded. "I thought you'd never ask."

They slipped out to the courtyard, peering over the wall to watch the River Severn as it swelled from under the bridge, a chill breeze still blowing. Tasha drew the DI close, thumbs caressing her cheeks.

"Can you believe we finally did it?" she whispered. "I was always worried I would never get you here."

Yvonne shook her head. "I'm pinching myself." She pulled back her head to study Tasha's face. "I know it hasn't been easy. But we were always going to make it."

The psychologist nodded, tucking stray strands of blonde hair behind Yvonne's ear. "And we'll keep making it... One day at a time."

They watched the river, breathing in tandem as the distant sound of music drifted from the reception hall. Tom came to see where they were, waving at them from the doorway.

Yvonne grinned. "I believe that's our cue, Dr Giles."

"Why yes, I believe it is, Mrs Phillips," Tasha grinned.

Yvonne placed her hand in the crook of her wife's arm as they made their way across the courtyard and up the stone steps.

THE HEAVY DOOR of the reception venue swung open, and they were back amid the celebrations. Tasha headed to the bar.

Yvonne, taking her seat at the table, sensed a shift in the air; a subtle dissonance in the previously carefree atmosphere. Thumping music clashed with the tension she witnessed on the faces of the DCI and Dewi as they chatted at the table next to her. The sergeant's usually relaxed posture was stiff, concentration lining his forehead.

The DI's brow furrowed as her gaze swept the room,

lingering on each member of the team. Callum, leaning against a wall with his arms crossed, avoided eye contact, his usual smouldering intensity replaced by an inward focus. Dai also seemed preoccupied. And DCI Llewelyn kept looking at the clock, his face more weary in the pale sunlight entering through large windows.

"Something's off," she whispered to Tasha, who had returned with their drinks. "Give me a moment... I'll be right back."

She strode over to her sergeant as the DCI left for the bar. "What's going on, Dewi?" She asked, a gentle hand on his arm.

"Ask me tomorrow," he murmured, his serious tone clashing with the surrounding merriment. "This is your special day."

"It can wait," Callum joined them, placing another pint in Dewi's hand.

"Where's your lovely wife?" Dai asked, attempting to change the subject.

"What's going on?" she demanded, put out that everyone seemed to know what the matter was except her. "What's happened?"

The DS shook his head. "I'll get you another drink."

"Dewi?"

DCI Llewelyn walked over. "It's not good news, Yvonne," he said, his voice low. "But given the circumstances..."

"You might as well tell me. I can see from your faces there's a problem." Her voice was calm, but firm. "I won't rest until I know."

Dewi shifted the weight between his feet, looking torn.

Callum ran a hand through his hair, while Dai shrugged apologetically.

"Step over here a minute," Llewelyn suggested, nodding towards a less occupied corner of the room.

She swallowed hard as she followed him. The clink of glasses and the sound of laughter faded into the background.

3

BODIES IN THE FOREST

Yvonne stood motionless, her back to the revelry, instincts bristling at a secrecy she thought pointless. "What is it?" she pressed, her voice firm, "I can handle bad news… I got married… I didn't morph into someone else."

"Earlier today, a farmer found three bodies in the woods near Dolfor." DCI Llewelyn's face was dark as granite from the Cambrian Mountains.

"Oh, no…" She frowned. "Are we talking murder?"

"As it stands, the deaths are unexplained. But the circumstances are suspicious."

"Where were they found?"

"Off the steep cut-through road from Newtown," Llewelyn rubbed his forehead, voice hushed. "The dead men had abandoned their car at The Dingle. It left the road, presumably because they hit the corner too fast. Ended up in bushes. It would be straightforward death by misadventure, except their bodies were nowhere near their trashed vehicle. They had wandered a considerable distance away before succumbing." His words hung like the mist that had shrouded the valley that morning.

Yvonne frowned. "Have they identified the bodies?" she asked, her mind already mulling over the potential investigation, if foul play were to be confirmed.

"They think the men are those from Newtown who went missing last weekend, and hope to have confirmation by this afternoon," he replied, expression grave. "If it is them, we know they were drinking at a pub in town for several hours. We don't have confirmation yet whether the driver was drunk. I will organise what's needed. I'm sorry about the secrecy I thought you should be—"

"Kept in the loop... always," she finished for him, knowing that it wasn't what he was about to say. She understood their desire to protect her on her wedding day, but they were a team. And, although today had been for other vows, her oath to serve had never wavered.

"Fine," the DCI nodded. "We'll brief you first thing in the morning."

"Good." Her shoulders relaxed; her voice softening. "I'll explain to Tasha, but we had to delay our honeymoon until the summer, anyway, because of a pressing case she has in London. It will be fine."

Yvonne's gaze missed nothing as she scanned the briefing room, focussing briefly on each member of the team. The clatter of mugs and shuffle of papers diminished to a hushed expectancy as all eyes moved to the maps and aerial photographs projected onto the wall behind her. She attached three photographs to the map. "Ben Davies,

Thomas Howells, and Hayden Pryce," she began, pointing at the images of the deceased as she named them. Three lives tragically cut short. "Who were they? And what's their story?"

The team committed the victims' faces to memory.

"First, do we know who found them?" she asked.

"A local farmer," Dewi replied. "Yesterday morning… He was out looking for lost sheep with his dogs near Dolfor. He's given a statement."

"What about the families?" she asked, thinking of the grief that would have come with a knock on the door. These were not simply names or numbers; they were sons, brothers, and future fathers. And somewhere out there, people had waited for them to come home, unaware they never would. She had witnessed such crushed souls many times. It was one of the hardest parts of the job.

"Uniformed officers informed them yesterday, ma'am, after the victims' identities were confirmed."

Callum nodded. "Ben Davies was eighteen years old. Thomas Howells was twenty. Hayden Pryce was nineteen. All were from the Newtown area. Ben was training to be a carpenter. He was well-liked locally. Thomas Howells worked for the local forestry commission, his family having moved from Cardiff two years ago. And Hayden Pryce, the youngest, was a university student in Aberystwyth studying environmental science. He was home with his parents for a month. Ben and Hayden had been friends since infancy. Thomas's family lived close to Ben's, and the three lads became best friends." He put his notes down. "We don't know why they drove that way after drinking, or why they were in the woods after the crash. Their bodies were not found together. They were several hundred metres apart from one another. It is an isolated area with dense woodland that hikers and locals sometimes visit, but they wouldn't usually go there after dark."

"What about the car?"

"The vehicle was discovered in bushes near the Dingle. It's a write-off. It side-swiped a tree as it left the road, coming to rest amongst the undergrowth. Must have been a fair impact. The men likely succumbed to their injuries and the cold. The big question is why were they found so far from the crash site?"

Yvonne pressed her lips together, witnessing the injured men running in fear in her mind's eye. "It says here," she pointed to Hayden's photograph, "this man was absent his footwear."

Callum nodded. "That's right."

"Have they found his shoes yet?"

"Not to my knowledge."

"Don't you find that odd?"

The DC shrugged. "They could have come off while he was running away in confusion after the accident? The undergrowth is pretty dense in places. The shoes may be there, just not discovered yet. They plan to take dogs up there later today."

"Something is not adding up..." The DI placed her hands on her hips. "Three young men go drinking in Newtown, get into a car, and drive out of town in the opposite direction from where they live. Their vehicle crashes into trees after leaving the road and they abandon the car and wander off, away from the safety and town and home... all in freezing conditions. Why would they do that?"

"As Callum says, they became disoriented after the crash..." Dai frowned. "Though, I admit, their actions were highly unusual."

"Perhaps the driver was worried about getting into

trouble and didn't want to risk losing his licence? It wouldn't be the first time a driver under the influence has walked off before police had a chance to speak to him." Callum sat back in his chair, folding his arms. "Though it is odd that all three ran uphill. Especially nursing injuries like that."

Yvonne allowed that thought to settle like sediment before continuing. "I think we should go up there and look around. Perhaps it *was* a tragic accident, but something about this whole incident feels off. I won't be happy until we've examined the scene for ourselves, and received the postmortem results."

4

EVERY MARK TELLS A STORY

Yvonne and Dewi were at pathologist Roger Hanson's office at the mortuary to discuss the injuries the three young men had sustained, and to confirm their cause of death.

"All the bodies bore signs of trauma." Hanson handed photographs to the two detectives.

Yvonne pursed her lips, studying the images. Bruising, scrapes, and cuts marred each of the victims' pale skin. Whatever their reason for running, they must have done so in a great deal of pain.

"Although you see multiple lacerations and contusions, these injuries would not have been fatal on their own. They were not bleeding out. However, the shock after the crash would have dilated blood vessels, and they would have lost body heat faster as a result. That night was bitterly cold. We are talking minus ten degrees. Add to that the wind chill, and you can lower it another several degrees. They had dressed for a night in the pub, not a saunter through local forestry."

Yvonne frowned, peering at the photos. "Would you say

these injuries were consistent with the crash? Could they have resulted from violence by another party?"

"It's possible." Hanson sat back in his office chair. "But there isn't an injury I can point to, and say that a third person inflicted it. The search team didn't find any weapon at the scene. Although some wounds resulted from blunt force trauma, the crash could explain them. And the abrasions were to be expected, especially as the men exited a crashed car and ran through woodland. Running through rough terrain in the dark would likely result in cuts and abrasions, anyway. There were traces of paint and glass embedded in their clothing and hair, along with leaves and twigs — all consistent with collision debris."

Yvonne nodded. "Forensics found high levels of alcohol in Ben and Thomas's bloodstream. Hayden had a low level, suggesting he had consumed maybe one or two pints. We believe he was the driver."

"DRINKING, confused, and likely scared out of their wits," Hanson shrugged. "Panic can make people act illogically."

"Have you sent us a copy of these?" The DI handed back photographs that had left little to the imagination. Each abrasion, each discoloured welt, told their own tale of shock and pain.

"I have included everything in my report, which I am finishing this morning. I can get it to you this afternoon."

"Thank you. The bodies were located a considerable distance apart. Their ordeal spanned a large area. Maybe a mile or more? They became separated during the events leading up to their deaths. We are still getting our heads around why they ran in the direction they did, and what made them split up like that. I believe something scared them. Something stopped them from staying with the vehicle and phoning for help, or heading back towards town. They had their phones with them, but did not call emergency services. It's odd, to say the least. The crash site was only a quarter of a mile from town and safety."

"I agree... that *is* odd." Hanson nodded. "And I am surprised they made it miles from their vehicle in those temperatures, when they were in shock and pain. Perhaps they *were* running from someone, after all. It could, of course, be the phenomenon of mass hysteria, where one member of the group convinces everyone else that something dreadful is about to happen, maybe out of delirium resulting from injuries?"

Dewi shifted in his seat, opening the buttons on his tweed jacket. "They crash, stumble out of their vehicle, and instead of calling for help or going back to the road, they bolt into the trees... I agree with Yvonne. I think something else happened after the crash. The question is, what?"

THE WHEELS of their unmarked vehicle crunched over loose gravel on the tarmac as it snaked towards The Dingle, a dell surrounded by dense foliage, running parallel to the cut-through. If you blinked, you would miss it. Yvonne surveyed the scene, cataloging details like a chess player contemplating the board. Beside her, Dewi drove in silence, looking for a convenient place to park.

As they peered down from the lane, after leaving their vehicle at the side of the road, she felt the hairs rise on the back of her neck on seeing the remains of Hayden Pryce's battered blue Subaru. She couldn't imagine those boys powering up the windy, narrow lane with enough speed to end up how and where they did. Something wasn't right.

The twisted carcass of metal and shattered glass ensnared in the bushes below provided testament to the violent ending of the young men's journey out of town. A blue-and-white police cordon flapped in the breeze.

"Let's take a closer look," she said, eyes still on the wreckage.

"Right behind you." Dewi pressed his fob to lock the car.

They got as close as they could to the wreckage, breath forming vaporous clouds in the frosty air.

Yvonne approached the scarred tree first, its bark gouged away where the vehicle made its desperate impact. The grooves were deep, jagged lines indicating a high velocity glancing blow. Her fingers traced the edges, reconstructing the story told by the wounded bark with blue paint chips embedded. "Look at this," she called to the DS, motioning him closer. "The force of the impact must have been considerable."

He nodded. "The driver didn't stand a chance of correcting their course." His words lingered in the stillness of the surrounding trees. "Makes you wonder what made them drive so fast on this road, doesn't it?"

"Or who?" Yvonne answered, her brows knitting together. She stepped back, surveying the crash site with a critical eye. The vehicle was a write-off, every panel buckled or torn, the interior contents lying scattered amongst a mess of tiny glass shards.

"They found two of the lads' phones lying in the vehicle." Dewi put his hands on his hips. "Hayden's, and Thomas's. Ben Davies' phone was lying close to his body in the woods."

"Odd, isn't it?" Yvonne answered. "They run uphill, away

from safety? And not even a call for help? It looks like they exited the vehicle in a hurry."

"Maybe they were afraid it would explode," Dewi offered. "Though there wasn't a fuel leak, as far as I can tell. They were getting quite low on petrol."

"Yes, that might explain the quick exit." Yvonne's lips pressed into a thin line, her gaze fixed on the hedges and trees behind which the town lay hidden. "But my instincts tell me there's more to this than shock and poor judgment."

"Well, your intuition has proven correct more than once," he agreed. "Maybe toxicology will give us some pointers."

"Let's make sure we get a good look at the car before they haul it off for examination." She took out her mobile and snapped a few pictures.

The surrounding woods seemed to close in, silent witnesses of the events that unfolded that fateful night. Each bent twig or disturbed patch of earth held teasing clues to the questions burning in the DI's mind. She was determined not to miss a single detail, knowing justice for the three men might depend on it.

A PREGNANT SKY LOOMED OVERHEAD, as though more snow might fall at any moment.

The detectives climbed back into their car and headed further up the lane to the woods in which the men had died, travelling via the fateful bend from where the victims' vehicle left the road. Black rubber stained across the tarmac told of a desperate attempt to control the car, a chaotic pattern born of panic.

They got out to examine the skid marks; the DI crouching; her mind retracing the violent swerve that had taken the vehicle from the road and into the undergrowth. "They braked hard right before the turn," she murmured, her fingertips brushing over the ground as if to glean truth from the cold asphalt. "It's like they were…"

"Chased," Dewi finished for her, his eyes scouring the road. He stood a few paces back, arms folded across his chest, the fabric of his suit stretching tight over his broad shoulders.

"It's something we should consider," Yvonne said, standing upright. "Though we can't discount youthful bravado, and the driver showing off; pushing the limits." Her voice held no judgment, only experience from having seen such tragedies in the past.

The pair exchanged a knowing look before climbing back into their car and driving on to the edge of the wood, where they left the vehicle, to continue on foot.

Silence shrouded the scenes where each of the bodies was found, except for the fluttering of police tape, hanging like a morbid bunting in the breeze.

They walked to where Ben Davies had lain, clothing awry amidst the bracken and rotted leaves. A photograph they had taken with them showed his body lying twisted, as though he had fallen while running. It spoke of his frantic dash through the unforgiving terrain. Yvonne pulled out a small voice recorder to document her thoughts. "The more I see, the more I am convinced something made them run up here," she said to Dewi. "I think they were terrified."

"I think you may be right," he agreed.

"Let's move on to the next." She pushed her hands deep into the pockets of her long cream coat, the chill wind penetrating her bones as they picked up pace to the next scene.

Dewi eyed the thicket where Thomas Howells had collapsed, before comparing it with the photograph in his hands. "It is hard to see how even disorientation after the accident could lead them so far up here. They had to know they were heading up into the hills, and not down towards town."

She nodded. "And how did they come to be so far apart from one another? Did they split up to improve their chances of escaping? If so, what? What were they running from?"

"If someone chased them from town, perhaps the pursuers continued into the trees after them." Dewi scanned the surrounding landscape.

She nodded. "Let's hope SOCO found some trace of them, if so."

Finally, they arrived at the place where Hayden Pryce had lain.

"Here…" Yvonne handed Dewi another photograph. The image was of Hayden Pryce's body, his boots missing. "Search teams with dogs have scoured the woodland between here and the vehicle, but they have still not found his footwear."

"Odd that," he muttered, gaze flitting between the photo and the forest floor. The detritus-littered ground showed no sign that a body had ever been there, save for the cordon erected only days before.

"It doesn't make sense, does it?" She mulled over the grim irony. "Newtown's lights would have been visible from the edge of the trees, but the dead men opted for a treacherous climb in frigid conditions. Keep looking," she instructed. "Evidence doesn't lie, and neither do the dead. We simply have to listen."

. . .

Her boots crunched on frosted undergrowth as she looked for the paths taken by the victims on their bizarre flight.

The DS matched her stride, eyes scouring the ground for signs other searchers may have missed.

"Look at this," the DI pointed at thin branches which appeared newly snapped. "Looks like one of them may have run this way."

Dewi grimaced. "Maybe they were under the influence of more than alcohol?"

"It's certainly possible." Yvonne squinted, picturing the scene. "What else might we be missing?"

"Perhaps the answers don't lie here," he replied, breath forming clouds in the frozen air. "Maybe something happened while they were at the pub?"

"Ben and Thomas had dishevelled and torn clothing." She mused aloud, her voice barely above a whisper. "And Hayden, without his shoes... running, stumbling... It must have hurt. I agree, Dewi, perhaps they *had* used substances which resulted in a bad trip. We've seen that before."

"Shall we push on?" Dewi asked, checking his watch. "I left Callum to organise interviews for this afternoon and tomorrow. We ought to be getting back soon."

She nodded. "I'm almost finished."

Twigs snapped underfoot as they navigated the uneven terrain into a gully, going deeper into the woods that had swallowed three young men. The cold had a firm grip on the forest, frosting over budding wildflowers and detritus alike. The DS trailed behind.

"I don't get it..." she muttered to herself, stopping abruptly, head cocked to one side.

"Ma'am?" He caught up, but knew better than to disrupt her train of thought when she was like this.

Her gaze remained fixed on the tangled shadows

between the trees. "The human mind grasps for survival; it clings to hope. Why did they not seek light, noise, people? Instead of cold and darkness?"

"Maybe they couldn't," he offered.

"Exactly..." The DI continued walking, eyes scanning the undergrowth. "Something drove those boys to their deaths. It's up to us to find out what." She drew her long coat tight against the biting wind. "Right, Dewi, let's back to the car."

5

THE DRUNKEN WITNESS

An unshaven and dishevelled Dilwyn Jenkins sat in interview room two, mumbling to himself. An odious stench suggested he was hungover and had not washed in days. It stung the DI's throat, and she coughed, wishing she had left the door several inches ajar.

She placed her notepad and papers down on the table and took a seat. "Thank you for coming in, Mr Jenkins." She glanced through her notes as his red eyes appraised her. "I understand you were up at The Dingle on Friday night, and in the early hours of Saturday morning?"

"I got myself in a bit of bother, didn't I," the grey-peppered, fifty-one-year-old answered, his voice gruff. He rubbed his long, wayward eyebrows as though nursing a headache. "That's it, now... I'm on the wagon. No more drinking for me... That was the last time. I should have stopped years ago." He dropped his hands from his face. "How long is it till I get my licence back? Two years?"

"Something like that." She pressed her lips together. "Drink-driving is a serious offence, Mr Jenkins. But you knew that before choosing to drive a car to the pub in

Dolfor and consume several pints before attempting to drive home again. You took your vehicle with the full intention of driving after drinking. You must have known that getting caught would mean losing your licence, but you did it anyway. It was all premeditated. But that isn't why I asked you here today."

His face tightened, a muscle flicking on his cheek as he leaned back in his chair.

"I asked you here because you abandoned your vehicle on the Garthowen estate after you had scraped several parked cars with it."

He flinched, groaning, and began rubbing his forehead once more.

"And there was a serious accident on the cut-through road you used to get back to town. The car was a write-off. Why Garthowen?"

"What do you mean?"

"You don't live in Garthowen. Why did you turn off from your route home and abandon your car on the first estate you came to?"

He grunted, clearing his throat as though showing a doctor his tongue. "I knew I shouldn't be driving in that state. I thought I was limiting the damage."

"Really?" she studied him, her blue eyes taking in every micro-expression. "You see, I thought it might have been because you narrowly avoided crashing into another vehicle near the Dingle, and saw that car leave the road and plunge into trees."

"No-"

"It shook you up so bad, you abandoned your car at the first opportunity, not wanting to be associated with an accident you assumed had been fatal."

He shook his head. "Everything you said there is nonsense."

"How many times have you driven after consuming alcohol? Two hundred? Five hundred?"

He frowned. "It was my first time."

"Really? Do you know the statistics for the average number of times a person has driven drunk before being caught for it?"

He pulled a face.

"Two hundred, Mr Jenkins. Two hundred times." She laboured the last three words for effect.

"Well, I was really unlucky, then, wasn't I?" He folded his arms, scowling at her. "Because that was my first time."

She sighed, pursing her lips, spreading papers with one hand. "It's quite a coincidence, you coming down that road under the influence, and another vehicle swerving off that same lane and ending up in undergrowth."

He shrugged. "Coincidences happen. That's why they call them coincidences. Those boys were probably drunk as well... That's why they came off the road. It's probably why they were on that road. It's quiet. Less chance of getting caught by police."

"Is that why you were on that road?"

"No."

"Then why assume that was why they used it?"

He shrugged. "Because some people do that."

"The driver of the crashed vehicle was sober."

He shrugged, grunting and mumbling something she couldn't quite catch.

"You said, 'boys'."

"What?"

"Before... You said, 'those boys were'..."

"So what if I did?"

"How did you know who was in the other car? How did you know it was boys, plural?"

"Everybody's talking about it... the vehicle that crashed at The Dingle. They said the lads ran off into the woods and died in the snow."

"And you didn't see it happen?"

He mumbled incoherently.

"I'm sorry?"

"I want a solicitor."

"Very well, Mr Jenkins. This interview will continue in a little while, as you have now changed your mind, and would like a solicitor to be present. Interview suspended, two-fifteen pm." She gathered her papers. "An officer will bring you a cup of tea while you wait."

"My client would like to change his statement." Darren Bayliss, Jenkins' solicitor, announced.

"Very well..." She nodded. "Does he know the consequence of wasting police time?" She exchanged glances with Dewi, seated next to her.

"He does, and he says he's serious." Bayliss nodded. A lock of cream-slicked hair fell forward. He hand-combed it back into position.

"Fine..." The DI kept her tone firm and even.

"Dilwyn informs me he did see the boys after their accident, after all."

"He did?"

"Yes, but he did not witness the accident itself, only the boys staggering back onto the lane as he was coming down it."

"Did you collide with them?" she asked Jenkins directly.

"No, I was going real slow because I'd been drinking, and the weather was bad. There was snow and ice. I was taking it steady."

"Where did you see the lads, exactly?"

"They were scrambling up the embankment next to the Dingle, onto the lane. Their sudden appearance scared me. I thought they were up to no good. I thought they might try to car-jack me."

"Why didn't you tell us this before?"

"I don't know... I've been in a state since getting caught for drink-drive. And when I heard about... Well, that they died. It shook me up, like."

"What did you do when you saw the men climbing up onto the road?"

"I swerved round them and drove on a little further before stopping."

"Is that the truth?"

"Yes." Jenkins looked at his solicitor, as though expecting Bayliss to back him up.

"Did you see where the boys went next?"

He shrugged. "As far as I could tell, from my rearview mirror, they wandered up the road."

"You don't know where they would have been going or why?"

"No."

"What did you do next?"

"I carried on driving down the hill."

"You didn't call emergency services?"

"No, I had no reason to, did I? I didn't know there had been an accident. You can't see the wreckage from the lane unless you walk right up to the hedge and peer down."

"How would you know that?"

"My son told me after he had driven that way to look."

"So, you continued driving towards home, but abandoned the car in Garthowen. What made you do that?"

"I had to. It shook me up, seeing those lads just appearing on the road like that. I was feeling vulnerable, and the worse because of the drink."

"How did you get back home?"

"I telephoned my wife, as soon as I got back to Garthowen, for a lift. She picked me up. That was a couple of hours after I last saw the three men. It was bloody cold, I can tell you."

"I see..."

"I'll lose my licence, won't I?" He looked annoyed at that fact.

"You will. But then, as discussed previously, you knew that might be the consequence when you drove that night. And you were sober when you made that choice. You took the car to Dolfor village when you could have phoned for a taxi."

He scowled. "It's the waiting I don't like. Taking you there is fine. But last thing at night, when you phone for your return, it could be an hour before you can get your ride home."

"But then, surely, you phone for your return an hour before you need it, don't you? Or you pre-book your return?"

"Then the night goes on longer, and you don't want to go when the taxi turns up."

The DI pressed her lips together. She could not win this one. He evidently had a long line of excuses and justifications. He could go through them with the tutors on the drink-impaired driver's course at probation. They would sort him out. "And your wife will confirm what you have told me, will she?"

"She will."

"Was it your wife who drove your car back to town?"

"My wife and a friend, yes."

"And your wife's friend's name?"

He shrugged. "You would have to ask her."

"Very well." Yvonne gathered her papers together. "I think we are done here."

"I saw an SUV go up the lane. It passed me as I was on my way down."

The DI frowned. "What time would that have been?"

"I don't know… Maybe one in the morning."

"What SUV? Do you know the model? And colour?"

"It was a dark night, but it looked dark-blue or maybe black. More likely dark-blue. I didn't notice the make or model."

She made notes. "Thank you… One more thing before you go," she added. "Did you notice whether all the men were wearing their shoes when you saw them on the road?"

He shook his head. "I didn't look at their feet."

"Fine…" She sighed. "I want you to let us know if you remember anything else about that night. Something you haven't already told us. Three men died that evening, and we want to know why."

"I don't get it…" Yvonne frowned as she walked back to CID, accompanied by Dewi. "He drives home but, after seeing three men scramble up the bank onto the road, he changes his mind, abandons the car, and rings his wife. I think he is leaving something out. Something vitally important."

The DS rubbed his chin. "But he said their sudden appearance scared him. He thought he was going to be carjacked. Maybe it really did scare him enough to abandon the car and call his wife?"

"But why continue on towards the town. Why not leave the car in a layby and phone his wife to pick him up from the lane?"

Dewi pursed his lips. "I don't think he's telling us everything he knows."

"I agree." Yvonne nodded. "I think we'll be talking to him again."

6

WHO WERE THE POWYS THREE?

The late afternoon sun cast a warm glow over Old Canal Road as Yvonne and Dewi pulled up at the Davies's family home. A modest two-story cottage, it wore a coat of peeling paint and the weary posture of several years inattention. Yvonne adjusted her coat, bracing for a wind that was bending saplings in the neighbour's garden, and mentally preparing herself to speak with Ben's grieving family.

Dewi knocked on the door.

A man in his late forties, with greying hair and a square jaw, opened it.

"Mr Davies?" she asked, her gaze and voice soft. "I'm DI Yvonne Giles, and this is DS Dewi Hughes. We are so sorry for your loss."

He led them down a short hall to a narrow sitting room, where he sat next to his wife on the sofa, after settling the officers in armchairs. A fire cracked and spat in the grate.

The DI felt for the couple, noting their pale pallor, and the way they leaned into each other in a united front against a world that had snatched their son away. A lump formed in her throat.

"Thank you for coming," Beryl Davies murmured, clutching a tissue crumpled beyond further use. "We can't believe Ben's gone... he was always so full of life. This place is empty without him."

Yvonne took out her notebook. "Tell me about him. Tell me about your son."

Adjusting the scatter of faded cushions behind his back, Dai Davies cleared his throat, his voice rugged with emotion. "Ben was never one to shy away from hard work," he said. "He put in long hours at the workshop, always looking to learn something new. He took pride in the things he did."

"Thought he might open his own workshop one day," Mrs Davies interjected, a wistful look on her tear-stained face. "He had big plans. Ever since he was little, he watched his dad and uncles making furniture and working the lathe. He'd get stuck in, too. He'd come in, as little as he was, covered in sawdust and beaming from ear to ear; a chisel in one hand, and a planer in the other." She choked, a sob escaping her heaving chest.

Yvonne pressed her lips together, heart heavy for them.

"He'd recently met a girl... Emily," Mr Davies' brows knitted together. "Emily Wright... He seemed quite taken with each her. She might know more about what he was up to before... before that night. They had seen more of each other over the last month." He sighed. "Perhaps, if she had been out with them that night, none of this would have happened."

"Emily," Yvonne repeated, adding the name to her list of leads. "We will speak with her, thank you. Is there anything you can tell us about the events leading up to Ben and his friends going out that night? And do you know why they were travelling along the short-cut route to the Dolfor Hills? It's the other end of town from their homes. Does Emily live out that way?"

"As far as we know, Emily lives with her parents on a farm." Mrs Davies sniffed. "The farm is out that way, but Ben would never disturb her at nearly midnight. He was far too polite to do something like that. Besides, he would be too afraid of upsetting her parents. We don't know why he was up at The Dingle. We've talked about it, and it makes no sense to us. They would always come home when the pubs closed, or let us know if their plans changed for any reason."

"And they didn't make contact that night?"

"No, and that is very unusual."

The DI made notes before leaning forward, elbows resting on her knees. "Can you tell me about Ben's friends?" she asked, her voice gentle. "Were there any disagreements or conflicts between the group we should know about?"

"Not between Ben, Tom, and Hayden. They were as close as friends can be. They had each other's backs. No question about that." Dai Davies exchanged glances with his wife before continuing. "He had his workmates from the workshop. They'd go out for a pint every now and again," he said, his voice trailing off.

"Any problems there?" Dewi asked.

"There was an argument a few weeks ago." Beryl twisted the crumpled tissue in her lap. "A bit of a spat between Ben and a customer he did some work for. It was a disagreement over a repair job, apparently."

"Was it serious?" Yvonne made a note.

"I don't think so." Dai shook his head. "From what Ben said, it was a simple misunderstanding. The customer had given vague instructions, and Ben made the wrong adjustments or something." He flicked his head dismissively. "They sorted it out the next day. Ben wasn't one to hold grudges. I think he let the customer off without paying for the repair."

Beryl eyed her husband. She opened her mouth and closed it again.

"Still..." Yvonne's voice trailed off as she made a mental note of the look on Beryl's face. "Such issues can sometimes simmer below the surface. We'll look into it. Do you have the customer's name?" She asked, pen poised.

"Keith Miller. But honestly, Ben said they were back to civil conversation afterwards," he assured her, though a quiver in his voice hinted at anxiety.

"Is there anything else you think we should know?"

Dai and Beryl shook their heads.

"Very well." Yvonne closed her notebook with a soft thud. She stood, casting one last glance over the photographs of Ben at different ages that lined the mantle piece and book shelves. "Thank you for your time and for being so forthcoming. Once again, I am sorry for your loss. We will handle the investigation with the utmost care, and will update you as our inquiry progresses. Please let us know if you remember or hear of anything else you think we should know."

"We will, Inspector," Beryl said as Yvonne reached the door, her voice cracking with desperation. "I don't for one minute believe his death was an accident. Please find out why this happened to our boy?"

"We will do our utmost, Mrs Davies." Yvonne answered, her hand lingering on the doorknob. "I promise we'll leave no stone unturned."

Stepping into the crisp spring air, Yvonne turned to Dewi. "We have two new leads, Ben's girlfriend, Emily, and the customer, Keith Miller." She pursed her lips. "I think Ben's father is worried about something connected to Miller."

"I saw that, too." He nodded. "The name Miller rings a bell. I'll look him up."

⁓

THE BITING wind tugged at their coats as Yvonne and Dewi approached the Howells's family home, a two-up; two-down on Barnfields' estate, close to the Old Canal Road.

They knocked on the green door of the red-brick dwelling, and waited, Yvonne clasping her arms around herself for warmth.

A man in his mid-forties, his wife behind him, answered the door.

"Mr and Mrs Howells?" Yvonne showed her ID, her voice soft with empathy. "I'm sorry for your loss. May we come in?"

They followed the couple through to a tiny lounge heated by a gas fire that appeared decades old.

Yvonne took a seat on one end of the sofa, while Dewi sat on an old wooden chair near the door.

"Please know we are determined to uncover the truth about how Thomas and his friends met their deaths." She took out her notebook.

"It's all we can think about," Dave Howells replied, his voice hoarse. "We want to know why they died in that wood. They survived crashing their car. If they could run through the wood like that, they could have walked back down that road, surely..." His voice trailed off.

"We agree," Yvonne said, her voice gentle, sensing the father was teetering on the edge of losing composure. "We want those answers too, and will do everything we can to get them for you and Thomas."

"He was too innocent for this world." Tina Howells said, lower lip trembling; dabbing at her eyes with hanky. "But he had plans." Her voice sounded empty and distant. "He thrived outdoors, loved his work with the forestry commission. He said it made him feel... alive."

"He'd taken up hiking recently," her husband added, pride surfacing in his tone. "He said it cleared his mind. The three of them had been planning a trip up Snowdon in the summer."

Yvonne took notes. "Had they ever done anything like this before? Gone walking unexpectedly?"

"No, never." Tina Howells was adamant. "Tom never shied from a challenge. It was his nature to push himself. But he would never have gone off like that without telling us. They were responsible young adults. We gave them their space, but they knew we would worry if they were not home when they said they would be. Tom had done nothing like this before. It wasn't in his nature to leave us worrying. He knows I always wait up for him to come home."

"So he was adventurous and outgoing, but with a keen sense of responsibility." Yvonne reflected, taking in the essence of the young man whose absence had left an unbearable void for his parents. She observed their posture, the weariness etched into their features, the anguish in their voices.

"That was our Tom," Dave Howells agreed. "And that is the other thing. He didn't contact us at all. The last message we received was a text from the pub stating he would be home by midnight. There was no suggestion of his going off anywhere, least of all off out towards Dolfor. He did not need to be going out that way. None of them did."

"Do you still have the texts he sent you that night?" she asked.

"We do."

"Could I see them?"

Dave leaned forward to pick his phone up from the coffee table. "Sure." He flicked the screen several times. "There you go."

Yvonne read through the few messages sent by Tom that night, writing them down in her notebook. "Thank you for sharing these with us. It helps us to understand Thomas' intentions that night. It's the little details, added together, that will give us a fuller picture of what happened."

The couple appeared to take solace from her calm assurances. They nodded gratitude amidst their sorrow.

Yvonne paused before shifting the focus of her questioning, her gaze steady. "Tom's friends," she began, "did he ever talk about conflict within the group? Anything that might have been more than a passing disagreement?"

The Howells exchanged looks, a silent conversation passing between them before Dave cleared his throat. "Ben and Thomas were as close as you could get—like brothers since they were knee high. They had their moments, like all lads do, but nothing serious."

"No grudges that you know of?"

"None." Tina Howells affirmed, shaking her head with conviction. "They fell out on one occasion I can recall, when they were very young, over who owned a purple felt-tip pen. Both boys had received the same set amongst their Christmas presents and got confused. They couldn't have been more than six years old. But, even then, by the next day, it had all blown over. They were like brothers, always looking out for each other."

"And Hayden?"

Mr Howells shrugged. "They hadn't known him as long... Maybe a couple of years? But they had grown really close with him too, and there was never any trouble as far as I could see."

"Did Tom have a girlfriend?"

"He did... Sarah Lewis." Dave Howells rubbed his chin. "They were courting one other for a time. But they split up about a year ago. I think Tom had been hoping for a reconciliation, but she moved on, and Tom hasn't talked about her for over six months."

"Was he still in contact with her? Were they texting?"

"Yes, but only occasionally. Just checking in with each other, really. Their contact had dropped right off, as you would expect. I doubt they would have ever gotten back together."

"So she would be unlikely to shed light on what happened that evening?"

"I doubt she could be helpful." Mrs Howells murmured, uncertainty clouding her features. "But who knows? I guess I wouldn't want to rule anything out, really."

"Of course," Yvonne nodded in solemn acknowledgement. "We appreciate your openness at such a trying time. We will investigate every avenue and connection, however small, until we know the reason your son and his friends died in that wood."

As they left the Howells's home, Yvonne turned to Dewi, holding onto her hair to prevent it whipping her face. "I'll ask Callum to follow up on Sarah. Maybe she has a new boyfriend? I think it is unlikely the answers lie there, as they were no longer having much contact, but we shouldn't ignore the ended relationship. One of these pieces could be the key to unravelling what the hell happened that night."

GRAVEL CRUNCHED under the wheels of the unmarked police car as it rolled to a stop in front of the Pryce family's farmhouse in Aberhafesp, on the outskirts of Newtown. The sturdy and welcoming black-and-white structure nestled amidst sprawling fields. A gust of wind stirred the long grass, carrying with it the pungent scent of land fertilised with manure.

Yvonne stepped out, her gaze taking in a pastoral serenity that felt at odds with the sombre reason for their visit.

"Mr and Mrs Pryce," she began, her voice soft as she approached the grieving parents on their porch. "I'm DI Yvonne Giles and this is DS Dewi Hughes. I cannot express how sorry we are for your loss." Her eyes, so often analytical, were round with empathy.

"Thank you." Sian Pryce murmured, face gaunt; arms around herself for comfort or, perhaps, holding her son's memory to her.

Yvonne swallowed, knowing words could never fill the void left by their boy. "Please know we're doing everything possible to uncover what happened to Hayden and his friends. May we come in?"

They settled around an oak dining table in the farmhouse kitchen heated by a cobalt-blue Aga. The parents' eyes lost their hopeful spark as they realised there were no answers yet. They grasped each other's hands as they pulled chairs from under the long kitchen table and sat.

Yvonne listened as the couple painted a gentle portrait of their son.

Brian Pryce's voice cracked as he spoke. "Hayden had a heart as big as those fields out there. He was always helping, fixing things around here without being asked, and didn't like to see his mum stretching for anything or standing on stools. He would always jump up and help."

"His laughter filled our home," Sian Pryce added, her voice trembling. "And when he told us about the holiday job he had gotten at the bookstore, his eyes lit up with excitement. He loved reading and books, and we always understood he would go to university one day. When he became worried about global warming, he set his heart on environmental science, and studying for a doctorate after his degree."

"We want to know why he ended up running through that forest without his shoes." Brian Pryce's brow creased as his gaze fell to the carpet. "It makes no sense."

"Did you notice anything unusual about him or the other lads before that fateful night?" Yvonne asked. It was essential to keep the conversation focused, despite the pain it inevitably dredged up.

"Nothing out of the ordinary," Brian replied after a pause. "We were enjoying having him home for the holidays, and he seemed settled and relaxed."

"Did he ever mention new acquaintances or plans outside of work during his time here?"

"Only his regular catch-ups with Ben and Tom," Sian said, twiddling the edge of her cream jumper. "He loved those lads to bits. They were thick as thieves, they were."

"It sounds like they had a terrific friendship." The DI nodded. She surveyed the kitchen, as the tick of an antique grandfather clock echoed in the hallway outside of the open door. She leaned forward in her chair. "Mr and Mrs Pryce," she began, her voice gentle. "Can you tell us more about Hayden's social interactions? Did he ever complain about conflict with anyone, or did you notice changes in his behaviour before they left for town that night?"

The couple exchanged a weary glance, their features drawn tight with the pain of recollection. Brian cleared his throat, eyes clouded.

"Hayden has always been sociable. He loved being around people," he answered, his voice a low rumble. "He played football with his university team, and was looking for a team to play with around here during his time away from college. There was some disappointment at not finding one yet, but there was no trouble that we're aware of."

"That's right," added Sian, her hands clasped tightly in her lap. "Our boy was a peacekeeper. It's hard to imagine him embroiled in any sort of argument. He was always the one to calm things down if he witnessed people getting angry with each other. He was a quiet soul with a good heart."

"Thank you," Yvonne acknowledged, mentally filing away this small insight.

"Have you found his shoes yet?" Brian asked, eyes wide.

"Not yet..." Yvonne swallowed. "But searches are ongoing in the area. We have a dog team on it. If his footwear is out there, they have the best chance of finding it. They are the best at what they do."

The conversation continued for another twenty minutes, but there was little else Hayden's parents could tell them, aside from recounting stories of his boyhood and academic success. The detectives listened patiently. It never hurt to learn more about the victims. Sometimes, this information had proved to be the key.

Outside, the waning light of day bathed the farmhouse, while the fields beyond lay fallow and still. The DI worried they still had precious little to go on aside from the dodgy testimony of Dilwyn Jenkins, and the argument Ben Davies had with his customer Keith Miller in the weeks before his death. Still, that was a start. And a start was something.

THE CAR'S engine hummed in the dimming light as Yvonne drove with Dewi in the passenger seat. The air smelled of freshly turned earth from the fields as she turned on the heater.

"We should find out what happened at the pub that night. Maybe there's something we're missing." Dewi stared out of the window at the budding trees as they headed along the lane.

Yvonne nodded, her mind dissecting every word exchanged during the family visits. "I agree. We should find out where they were, and who they were with in the days before they died. I asked Callum and Dai to trawl through their texts, calls, and social media. I accept we may be wrong, and this may have been a tragic accident. But, if it wasn't, those boys deserve justice."

"I'll chase things with forensics." Dewi's gaze met Yvonne's.

"Thank you." She nodded. "And while we are at it, I think we should keep up the pressure on Dilwyn Jenkins. That man is as shifty as they come. And I think he knows more than he is telling."

THEY ARRIVED BACK at the station as the shadows lengthened and the sky bled into shades of crimson and purple. Yvonne's thoughts cast back to the families, and the strained hope, stoic resilience, and the raw anguish she had witnessed.

Each home was a microcosm of grief; a tableau of lives interrupted. But beyond the mourning, lay tantalising clues, each one a potential thread leading to the heart of what happened. She would begin by visiting the workshop where Ben Davies and worked, and argued with Keith Miller. Maybe Miller could tell them more about Ben, the argument, and perhaps even the events of that dreadful night.

She turned to the DS. "You said the name Keith Miller rang a bell earlier?"

Dewi frowned. "If it's the same Miller I'm thinking of, he has previous for dealing cannabis to friends."

"Really?" She pressed her lips together in thought. "Could that be why they were heading out that way? To pick up something from Miller? Where does he live?"

"If memory serves, he lives on a housing estate. Or, at least, his family did. It's been a while since I heard anything."

"We'll consider all motives," she nodded. "Jealousy, revenge, money, and drugs. If those lads were driven up those fields by fear, whoever frightened them did so with lethal intent. They must have known they might not make it in those conditions."

He nodded agreement, suppressing a yawn with his hand.

"Get a good rest." Yvonne smiled at him as they parted ways in the car park. "Tomorrow, we'll hit the ground running, and look into both Emily Wright and Keith Miller. We'll find out what uniform knows, if anything, about Miller's cannabis dealing. Perhaps he's into harder drugs, too. He could be the linchpin that breaks the case wide open. If he had something to do with those boys' deaths, I want him off the streets as soon as possible."

"Right you are, ma'am." Dewi yawned again as he waved goodbye. "I'll see you tomorrow."

As Yvonne's car rolled away from the station, the oncoming night embraced Park Street on her way through town. Streetlights reflecting off the windshield were welcome beacons as the darkness deepened. She was glad of them as she thought of Ben, Thomas, and Hayden's last hours in almost total darkness, and in freezing conditions. Their lives ended with their stories unfinished. But her team would not rest until they knew and understood their final chapter and served any justice warranted. That was her vow to the silent voices, and to the parents yearning for closure.

7

THE LAST DRINK

The heavy door of The Buck pub swung shut with a dull thud, as Yvonne and Dewi entered one of Newtown's oldest and most popular watering holes. An aroma of warm ale and wood smoke accompanied chatter and clinking glasses, as the detectives negotiated wooden tables on their way to the bar. Two young men playing pool looked up as the detectives approached. Not recognising the newcomers, their eyes returned to the game.

A group of four males and a female stood at the bar, where a middle-aged man with a gruff demeanour presided over the taps and bottles. Clive Owen had the build of one who was no stranger to hard work. His broad frame looked to have shouldered many a barrel in its time. He moved with practiced precision, pouring pints and exchanging banter, all while monitoring the lounge and those whose glasses were almost empty.

The DI's gaze swept the room, eyeing the flicker of the fire on varnished wood tables and the faces of the regulars. A subtle shift in the atmosphere was tangible as she and

Dewi approached the bar. She adjusted her jacket and cleared her throat.

The landlord, momentarily distracted from his task, regarded them with a discerning eye. His hands paused mid-pour.

"Afternoon," Yvonne said, her voice raised above the murmuring behind. It was a simple greeting, but enough.

He finished pouring the pint before setting the glass down in front of a customer. "How can I help?" he asked, throwing the bar cloth over his right shoulder.

"DI Yvonne Giles," she said, extending a hand.

The landlord's grip was firm, his hands rough.

"Busy day?" she inquired, nodding towards the punters at the tables.

Concern etched his weathered face as the DI leaned closer. "I'm fully licensed," he answered, his brow creased.

She grinned. "I'm not here to check your right to serve alcohol, Mr Owen. We're here to ask you about the three men who were found dead on the outskirts of Newtown, namely Ben Davies, Thomas Howells, and Hayden Pryce. We understand they drank here before driving out of town and crashing their car near The Dingle. A farmer found their bodies scattered in the woods. You must have heard about it?" She paused, giving him time, before continuing. "You may have known them? I'm told Ben and Tom popped in here most Friday nights."

He pulled the rag down off his shoulder and gave the polished wood a wipe. "I know those boys, yes. It was tragic what happened to them out there. They were probably dizzy after their car left the road like that. I'm amazed they were walking about after that crash, actually. I saw the photograph in the papers. It made a proper mess of their vehicle. How they wandered into the woods after that, I'll never know."

"The circumstances were odd." She nodded, the clamour of the pub receding into the background. "I was wondering if you remember anything from that night? How the boys were, their demeanour, and any interactions they may have had with others?"

"Em, let me see now…" He set his cloth down on the countertop, his rough-hewn voice matching the aged oak of the bar. "They had several pints here over a few hours. I wasn't the only one working here that night, but I served a couple of rounds for them, at least."

"How were they?" She inclined her head to better hear his reply, sensing the gears turning behind glazed eyes, as he mentally flicked through the memories of patrons served and drinks poured. "They seemed happy enough… mostly," he answered finally. "They were pleasantly merry, I would say. But one lad, the one I didn't really know that well, he had a couple of beers to start, and then drank coke for the rest of the time as far as I could tell. The other two knocked back a fair few pints altogether."

"Were they staggering when they left?"

"Not overly so, I wouldn't say. I mean, they must have had five or six pints each, but that was over two or three hours. I thought them intoxicated but not legless, if that makes sense?"

"You said they were happy, mostly. What did you mean by that? Were there problems during the evening? Any conflict? Heated arguments?"

He thought about it for a moment, his hands holding the rag, head inclined. "Nothing we had to call the police for." He shrugged. "The last couple of weekends have been really busy."

Yvonne's gaze lingered on him, her voice cutting through the din with practiced authority. "Are you sure? Think back to the night in question." Her brow furrowed. "Were there any incidents? Scuffles? Or words exchanged that caught your attention?"

His face contorted as he cast his mind back, rubbing the side of his face. "It was a fairly ordinary night," he responded finally. "We had the usual ebb and flow of punters until last orders." His fingers tapped a rhythmic motion against the cloth lying crumpled on the bar.

"Nothing out of the ordinary?" Yvonne pressed, doubting the evening would have passed off without at least one incident.

"Come to think of it..." A glint of recollection sparked in his eyes, "there was something that happened with Tony Jones." His fingertips stilled on the rag, and he leaned both elbows on the bar as though to sharpen the recollection. "He's a bit of a firecracker, is our Tony. Got into it with your victims over them pushing in at the bar."

Yvonne's posture straightened at the mention of Tony Jones. He was one of the town's less than savoury characters, who had tried his hand at several unlawful activities, but who always seemed to get off lightly by employing the area's best solicitors. She pulled out her notebook. "Describe the altercation, if you would."

"I wish I'd paid more attention early on, but I was pulling pints and bantering when the argument started. I know they exchanged angry words. If I remember rightly, Tony accused them of jumping the queue, and of thinking they were too good for the rest of them." His eyes darkened with the retelling. "The entire bar tensed up, like a storm was about to break. It went real quiet in here. That's when I paid proper attention to what was going on."

"So their argument was enough to quiet everyone in here?"

"Enough to turn heads, yes." Owen nodded. "But it didn't come to blows, not here, anyway. Still, for a few minutes, you could have cut the tension with a knife."

The DI and Dewi exchanged glances, aware that such an altercation might have continued after closing time. She wondered whether Tony Jones had decided to chase down the three young men after closing. It wouldn't have been out of character for the Newtown hard man. He worked out. His heft and muscular build would have been intimidating to slender young men.

Yvonne turned her attention back to the landlord. "What happened then?"

He leaned forward, hands gripping the edge of the bar. "They stood their ground, and so did Tony. For a moment, I thought it was going to turn nasty." His voice deepened. "There was a real tense moment."

"And then?" She observed the lines etched on his forehead, and the way his eyes darted to the floorboards where the incident had presumably occurred. "What was their behaviour like before they left?"

The landlord paused, considering with a deliberateness that matched the question. "There was no aggression, if that's what you mean. They seemed to shake it off after a bit. The lads were laughing again shortly afterwards. They seemed fine when they left."

"What about Tony Jones? Was he laughing? Chatting normally?"

"He seemed to settle back down, yes. Carried on bantering with his mates. He downed at least another couple of pints after that. I watched him for a bit, when I had the chance, and he showed no sign of aggression or anger afterwards that I could detect. Any bad blood seemed to have thinned out to nothing."

"Were there any girls with Ben, Hayden, or Tom that night?" She shifted position, her blouse sticking to her skin in the warmth of the packed room. This was not a good time for a hot flash.

"They were talking to a girl at one point." He scratched the stubble on his cheek, his gaze drifting towards the corner of the room, as though watching the conversation again. "She looked to be on a girlie night out, but seemed to know the boys well. They talked for a good half-an-hour, I would say. Couldn't tell you who she was, though. I can't say I'd seen her in here before." His tone held a hint of frustration as he glanced at his watch and at two people waiting to be served.

"You go ahead." Yvonne nodded towards the waiting punters. "We can continue afterwards."

"Maybe it was Emma White?" Dewi suggested to her, casting his eyes around the room.

"Exactly what I was thinking." She nodded. "Whoever it was, she may know more about what happened after the argument."

"Let's see if Clive knows her identity." He pushed his hands deep into his trouser pockets while they waited.

Owen turned his attention back to them.

"Can you describe the girl they were talking to? Any details you can remember could be helpful to us." Yvonne's keen eyes dissected every flicker of the landlord's expression, every shift in his stance, unsure whether he was holding something back.

"She was blonde, if I remember rightly. Though she could have been a brunette underneath. It was dim in here, and girls change their hair colour like they change clothes these days." His shoulders lifted in a half-hearted shrug. "But she was talking to the three lads, and the conversation seemed quite animated from the little I saw of it. I would say they all knew each other."

"Did you overhear any of the conversation?" Yvonne asked, her voice calm but insistent.

He squinted, pursing his lips. "I can't say I did. I'm sorry." He wiped the bar.

"Do you have any CCTV footage from that evening?"

"If we did, it's been overwritten. But I handed some footage in at Newtown police station when I heard what happened to the lads."

"Great, we'll hunt it down. Thank you for your help," she tapped the bar with her hand before producing a card from her coat. "If anything else comes to mind, anything at all, please don't hesitate to contact us."

"Will do." He pocketed the card with a nod, turning his attention to waiting customers.

YVONNE SQUARED her shoulders and followed Dewi out of the pub onto High Street. They mused over what Owen had said as they made their way to Broad Street and the car.

The stiff wind chilled her face as she buttoned her coat and put on leather gloves.

"Tony Jones isn't one for being messed with." Dewi pulled a face. "If he got it into his head that those boys needed teaching a lesson, I could imagine him following them after they left the pub."

"And if he was in a vehicle, he may have waited until they were clear of town to catch up with them."

"Exactly... He's roughed people up before. He's on a suspended sentence at the moment. He wouldn't have wanted to risk his freedom by being seen doing anything in public. But on a lonely road? With no eyes or cameras? It could be a different story."

"We need to find the girl they were talking to. Maybe she saw something."

"Or anyone else who might've seen the exchange between the boys and Jones," the DS offered, pulling out his phone to check messages. "The bar was busy that night. The landlord could have missed a lot."

"Indeed," Yvonne carried on walking. "The girl is crucial. We need to put a face to her as soon as we can."

"Facial recognition tech might give us a name when we get our hands on the surveillance footage from that night."

"Good thinking," Yvonne agreed. "We'll get Callum and Dai on it. I want every camera in the vicinity checked. If Jones followed those lads out of the pub, we should be able to confirm it with CCTV."

~

THE RIDE back to the station was quiet while Yvonne and Dewi mulled over what they had learned.

Callum approached them back in CID before they had time to take off their coats. "The DCI would like us to look into a disappearance." He flicked his head towards the back of the office. "Dai's over there, putting the kettle on. He thought you might need a brew. It's baltic again today." He grinned. "I'm glad I was in here."

"What disappearance?" Yvonne threw her jacket over the back of her chair.

The DC looked over his notes. "A twenty-two-year-old backpacker, name of Liam Stone, from Hull. He was on a four-week walking tour of Mid-Wales, and last contacted family and friends two weeks ago. According to his mother, he would not usually go more than a week without being in touch, and he often phones or texts more regularly than that. His parents are extremely concerned about not hearing from him."

"Last known whereabouts?" Yvonne frowned.

"Elan Valley, ma'am. But Newtown was on his list of places to visit, apparently."

"Where and when did he last access his bank account?"

"Dai is looking into that this afternoon. Should have an answer for us shortly."

"Good." She nodded. "We can begin progressing a search once we know what we are dealing with."

"One more thing..." Callum grimaced.

"Go on..."

"Dilwyn Jenkins is downstairs. He wants to give another statement about the night of the Dingle crash."

"Why?"

"Says he has remembered some more, ma'am. He wouldn't say anything else to me or the other officers. Said he wanted to tell you in person, and to make sure he got to speak to you specifically."

She sighed, looking at her watch. "Very well. I'll get myself sorted and go see him. Thanks, Callum." She shook her head. "Dilwyn Jenkins is a pain. What is the man playing at?"

Dewi pushed his hands into his pockets. "He was three sheets to the wind. I am not surprised he can't get his story straight. But he's the only eye witness we have of the boys up at The Dingle. I think we should push him today. Either he was so sozzled he can't remember, or he is up to no good. Either way, I don't think we should give him an easy time. If you want me there, that is?"

"Agreed, and I do." The DI grabbed her notes. "Let's find out what he is really about."

8

MIXED STORIES

Dilwyn Jenkins sat across from Yvonne and Dewi in the interview room, hands fidgeting atop the cold table. The fluorescent light, humming overhead, gave him a pallid sheen. He shifted in his chair, flicking a look sideways at the camera in the upper corner of the room.

"Let's go over it one more time, Mr Jenkins," the DI said, keeping her calm despite their principal witness's flakiness. "You are now saying the road was blocked that night?"

Jenkins nodded, swallowing audibly. His gaze settled on the jug of water in the middle of the table, avoiding eye-contact. "I was stuck for half an hour at least," he confirmed in a shaky voice. "I couldn't move the car because an SUV was stationary in the middle of the road. It was impassable on both sides."

"An SUV?" She cocked her head, eyes narrowed. "Is this the SUV you mentioned before?"

He didn't answer.

"You told us previously it came after you were stationary on the road?"

"Yes, but I remember more now."

"Tell me about the occupants," she sighed.

"I couldn't see them clearly, but they were talking to those three lads that died in the woods. At least, I think it must have been them, because I later saw at least five or six silhouettes in the SUV's headlights."

"Take me from when you arrived at the location, please."

"I pulled up when I saw the three lads scrambling up the bank. I slowed almost to a stop, and then the SUV arrived. Two or three people got out of that vehicle. The lads who had scrambled up the bank were talking with the people from the SUV. The discussion seemed... intense. They spoke in raised voices, but I couldn't make out what they were saying." Jenkins lifted a hand to his collar, adjusting it as sweat broke out on his temples.

"And then?"

"I needed a pee, and I got out of the car," he admitted. "I walked up to the hedge. There was a gate, and watched from behind it. I wasn't sure if the SUV's occupants intended on robbing those lads, and I feared becoming involved. I couldn't think straight. What with the beer and the fresh air, my head started swimming."

"What was happening on the road at this time?"

"I saw a bit of pushing and shoving."

"Between the two groups?"

"The guys from the SUV were pushing the three lads around. This went on for a bit, and then the lads took off into the woods like frightened rabbits." Jenkins' gaze stayed on the tabletop, where his fingers traced invisible patterns. "And I saw torches illuminating the trees, and zig-zagging along the road for a while before the SUV took off back the way it came."

"Anything else you remember?" She leaned forward, eyes scouring his face.

He hesitated, then shook his head. "No, nothing more. Just the car taking off and then silence. I drove to Garthowen shops and waited for my wife, Pat, to come pick me up. She and Ryan took me home. They were going to collect my car the following day."

"Ryan?"

"My son."

"How old is he?"

"Twenty, I think."

The DI made a note, her pen moving swiftly against the paper. She could hear Jenkins's laboured breathing, and tapped her pen against the edge of the table, the sound accompanying the low hum of the air conditioning. She sat back, gaze steady. "Dilwyn," she paused, lips pressing together, eyes piercing, "you've given us several accounts of that night, each differing from the last. Why didn't you mention this incident with the SUV blocking your way earlier?"

Jenkins shifted in his chair, eyes darting away before coming back to meet Yvonne's, sweat glistening on his brow despite the coolness of the room. "Well, my head was... it was all over the place that night." His voice wobbled. "The shock of finding out about the lads later muddled my thoughts even more than the drink. It was like trying to see through a fogged-up window. I didn't have a good memory to begin with, and I was shaken up, like. I'd been drinking. But now, bits and pieces are coming back clearer. I can make better sense of things."

"I see..." She allowed the words to hang in the air as she considered his response, dissecting every word, and weighing them against the things they had learned from other sources about the events of that night.

"It's less fuzzy," Jenkins affirmed. "I remember feeling uneasy, the SUV stopping in the middle of the lane, its engine idling, lights on full beam. And those blokes shaking down the lads. It made little sense at the time. But now…"

"Go on," Yvonne urged.

"Well, I think they must have intended harming those boys, don't you?"

"How do we know you are telling us the truth this time?"

"Look, I know how it seems," Jenkins continued, hands clasped together on the table. "But I swear the memory just wasn't there before. It's like pieces of a puzzle slowly coming together, isn't it? The memories have been gradually coming back. Now I remember crouching there, behind that gate, watching and wondering what was going down. I might have thrown up at one point, because I was feeling pretty rough. I was all disorientated, like."

Yvonne observed him intently, taking in his anxious rhythm, and the way his gaze flickered under scrutiny. Instincts honed by years of experience told her something was still not right with his testimony — a story that morphed with each iteration.

"Understand, Mr Jenkins, any detail, no matter how small, could be crucial. It's imperative that you're absolutely certain of what you recall. Wasting police time is a serious offence, as is obstructing the course of justice."

"I know," he replied, looking down again. "Look, I wouldn't say it if it weren't true. I'm telling you, I saw that SUV and it felt… ominous. And now the image of those men silhouetted in the headlights are stuck here," he tapped his temple, "like a photograph."

"Did you get the registration?"

He shook his head. "I couldn't have read it if I'd tried. And anyway, the people hid most of it because of where they were standing. I was glad when Pat and Ryan came to get me."

"Pat is your wife?"

"Yes, my wife and son came for me."

"You told us previously it was only your wife who picked you up?"

"Yeah, I forgot my son was there, too."

"Why did your son go along?"

"He came to drive my car back after I abandoned it in Garthowen."

"But he didn't collect the car. Was that because of the state it was in?"

"Yeah, I'd scraped a few parked cars. After I spoke with you last, I chatted with Ryan, and he said they stopped to check my car out, but decided they couldn't get it from there without causing more damage. "

"Very well," Yvonne scribbled on her pad. "We'll look into this SUV and attempt to verify your information."

"Of course," Jenkins exhaled, relief relaxing his features.

She stood. "We may wish to speak with you again, after we've had time to follow up on your statement. For now, you are free to go. DS Hughes will see you out."

She watched them exit; the door closing with a decisive click. She remained still for a long moment, contemplating the enigma that was Dilwyn Jenkins. The search for truth was often a labyrinthine exercise, but witnesses like the one she had just interviewed made things even more complicated. "Slippery as an eel," she mused aloud, gathering the rest of her papers.

. . .

Dewi rejoined her, shaking his head.

"What do you make of that?" she asked, running a hand through her hair and sighing.

"He's just asked me if his evidence will help get his license back. He thinks he can be let off his drink-drive offence."

She grinned. "He's got a nerve. I'll give him that."

"I think he's a few biscuits short of a packet." The DS tutted. "And I would think twice before believing a single word that comes out of his mouth."

Yvonne nodded, gathering her paperwork. "But what if he is right about the SUV? What vehicle does Tony Jones drive? I think we need to find out."

∼

A fine drizzle filled the air as they drew up in the carpark outside Tony Jones' home on Maesyrhandir estate. Although the weather had warmed, the damp made the DI shudder as they exited the vehicle.

"Do you see what I see?" Dewi placed his hands on his hips, eyeing the car parked opposite Jones' two-bedroom dwelling.

"A dark-blue SUV." She pressed her lips together, pulling out her mobile phone to snap photos of it from different angles. "No sign of any damage."

"No, it doesn't look to have been involved in a collision." The DS looked ahead at the house. A curtain twitched in the window. "Let's see what he has to say."

The lack of air in the small, square living room of Tony Jones' council house gave the home a stale stench, and likely contributed to the mould occupying a corner of the living room near the ceiling.

Jones' movements were stiff, his chest heaving intermittently. Sweat beaded on his brow.

Yvonne observed him across the threadbare sofa. His muscular frame appeared cramped in the modest space. The pale-brick estate loomed outside, and she could hear children playing in the distance.

"Mr Jones..." She flicked through her notebook. "We are here to talk about the evening of Friday, the fifth of March. Do you remember that night?"

Twenty-eight-year-old Tony shifted in his seat. Tight denim jeans creaked under the strain, and rolled-up shirtsleeves emphasised his large biceps. This, coupled with a stern countenance, signalled a readiness to fight, and a confidence he would win. His dark hair lay short and disciplined atop his head, though the stubbled jaw hinted at rebellion.

"Vaguely," he said, chin jutting out; a defiant light in his eyes. He looked at his watch, as though there was somewhere else he needed to be.

"Is that your car outside?"

"Which car?"

Her eyes narrowed. "The dark-blue Nissan."

"Nah, that's my brother Brandon's."

"Do you own a vehicle?"

He shrugged. "No need... I can use Brandon's whenever I like."

"Where is your brother?"

"He's at the gym. That's where I would be too if I didn't have to be here with you." He flicked his head, signalling frustration.

The DI lifted her wrist, pulling up her sleeve to expose

her watch. "It's two-thirty in the afternoon. Wouldn't you normally be at work?"

"We're between jobs."

"And what is it you do, Mr Jones."

He puffed out his chest. "Me and my brother are skilled labourers."

"I see."

Dewi observed in silence, his keen eyes missing nothing. He took off his jacket and scribbled something down.

"We understand you were drinking in The Buck that Friday, is that right?"

"Probably... We go there most Fridays, at some point."

"And you got into an argument?"

"Did I?"

"There was an argument in the pub and, according to witnesses, it became heated. You accused Ben Davies, Thomas Howells, and Hayden Pryce of pushing in at the bar while you were waiting to be served."

He frowned. "I don't like rudeness. One of them stood on my foot."

"It was an accident, surely?"

"They should look where they are going." He scowled. "I let them know exactly whose foot they had trodden on."

"Do you often throw your weight around?" She cocked her head, studying his face.

"When I need to... It's about respect." He leaned back, folding his arms.

"And you thought someone should teach them a lesson?"

"Look, what is this? They pushed in and trod on my foot. I told them off. That's it... No big deal."

"Where were you after leaving the pub that night, Tony?" She asked, her tone even.

"Here..." A sneer tugged at the corner of his mouth. "I came straight home, made a cup of tea, and went to bed."

"Did you travel home alone?"

"Brandon was with me, of course... He was driving." Tony shrugged, his eyes flitting to the window before locking back onto Yvonne's steady gaze, challenging her to prove otherwise.

She leaned towards him. "Another altercation occurred that night, following a road accident involving the three young men you challenged in the pub. Witnesses place an SUV similar to your brother's at the scene."

"Coincidence." Tony tossed his head, crossed arms like a wall between them. "I heard what happened to them. They must have got themselves into a bit of bother up there. I'm not surprised. They obviously had no common sense."

"That is harsh, under the circumstances." She frowned.

"Yeah, well, I'm sorry they died. I wouldn't have wished that on them, even if they were a pain in the-." He stopped himself.

"Are you telling me it wasn't you up there at The Dingle, confronting those boys after their car left the road?" Yvonne pressed. He was hiding something.

"You can't pin their deaths on me." He frowned, but perspiration made his forehead shine.

"We don't wish to pin anything on you, Tony," Dewi interjected. "We're trying to piece together what happened."

"Nothing happened. Not with me, anyway." He shrugged, but the movements were stiffer now.

Yvonne detected a faltering in the steely façade. "Truth has a way of surfacing, you know." She said, her voice soft. She watched a bead of sweat trace a path down his temple.

"Am I being charged with something? Because if you are

here to ask me about events I was not party to, I have somewhere to be."

"Like at the gym with your brother?" Her eyes didn't leave his. "Does it help when you throw your weight around? Does it achieve what you want it too. It's a lot to live up to, isn't it? A hard-man reputation? Do you get many challenges?"

Red-faced and fists clenched, he telegraphed barely suppressed anger. "I have nothing to say."

"Very well." She edged forward on the sofa as though about to rise. "But, before we go, CCTV footage shows you leaving The Buck at approximately eleven-thirty-five that night. That was a mere three minutes after Ben Davies and his friends departed." She noted the rigid jaw and pronounced rise and fall of his chest. He was stressed.

"Maybe it does..." He shrugged, unclenching his fists. "Coincidences happen."

"Just one of those things..." Dewi pursed his lips as he glanced at Yvonne. Both knew they had rattled him.

"CCTV shows your brother's SUV," Yvonne read from her notes, "turning left at the traffic lights by LIDLs supermarket, heading toward Garthowen, not long after. That was also remarkably close to the time those boys travelled that same way in their Subaru."

Tony's fingers tapped a staccato rhythm on the arm of the sofa. "So what? My brother goes all over town. It's a free country, last time I checked."

"Let's say I believe you," she said, eyes still on his face. "Where did you go after leaving the pub? If not towards the Dingle, then where?"

"We came home, via Garthowen."

"Okay..." She pressed her lips together. "So, let me get this straight... You leave the pub, climb into your SUV on

High Street and, instead of driving straight up the Llanidloes Road, taking a left off the roundabout, and down into Maesyrhandir, you instead take a left off the Llani Road, go along plantation lane, over many speed bumps, and round to Maesyrhandir, taking you significantly longer to get home."

"Yeah." His lips pressed into a thin line. "We took the scenic route."

She exchanged a glance with Dewi. Both knew he was stonewalling. It was time to change tactics. "Let's talk about who else was in the car, then... Keith Miller and Rob Lloyd. They left the pub with you, did they?"

"Obviously." He shifted uncomfortably, muscles tensing.

"Did Keith or Rob mention anything about their plans after leaving the pub? Where were they going?" She watched his eyes flicker, betraying a moment of uncertainty before the facade slipped back into place.

"We dropped them off at the bottom of Treowen Hill," he said, referring to the hill halfway between Llanidloes Road and Garthowen. "They're grown men. They do what they want."

"See, Tony, we've got a problem here..." Her tone was deceptively casual. "You've got no alibi aside from your brother, and he was in the SUV with you. We know you were travelling close behind the three young men you had argued with in the pub. And those men crash their car and later die in the woods. Doesn't look good, does it?"

"I told you, I went home." Tony's self-assurance faltered, his voice cracking.

"But nobody saw you return home at the time you said you did." Yvonne cleared her throat. "You could have been anywhere that night. Including the Dingle lane, when Ben, Tom, and Hayden got into trouble. Did they speed up to get away from you? Did you speed up? Were you chasing them? Is that why their vehicle left the road?"

"I told you, I wasn't there!" Tony spat the words through gritted teeth, hands balling into fists again.

"Let me be more specific." She sighed. "We have a witness who states a dark-coloured SUV, similar to your brother's, parked in the lane above the Dingle. The occupants of that vehicle had an altercation with Ben, Tom, and Hayden, right after their car crashed into The Dingle."

"How many SUVs are in Newtown?" Tony snapped, glaring at the DI. "There are plenty, that's how many. You are pissing in the wind. Those lads crashed their car because they'd been drinking and were likely going too fast for that road."

"Sure, except the driver was well under the legal limit, as testified by the staff at The Buck, and forensics."

"Maybe he took something," Tony fired back, arms crossed, biceps tensing.

"What do you mean? Do you know something?"

"Well, everyone knows those boys smoked weed. That Davies lad owed money, so I've heard."

"Owed who money? You?"

"I don't have nothing to do with that shit." He scowled.

"Then who?"

"Ask around," Tony suggested with a shrug. "Could've been anyone."

"Keith Miller?" She studied his face. "Did Ben owe Keith money? Was Keith looking for him that night?"

A muscle twitched in his jaw. He glanced away before meeting her gaze once more. "I have no idea." He looked at his watch. "I have to go."

"Very well..." She rose from the sofa. "Thank you for your time, Mr Jones. We'll be in touch."

. . .

"He knows more than he's saying." Dewi buttoned his suit jacket as they headed to the car.

"Did you see how he reacted when I mentioned Miller? And Ben Davies owing him money?"

"I did." The DS nodded. "I think it's time we talked to this Keith Miller."

"My thoughts, exactly."

9

THE DRUGS ANGLE

Keith Miller sat across from Yvonne and Dewi; lean frame hunched; feet fidgeting under the table. His shoulder-length hair, tied back in a rough ponytail, looked in need of a wash, a comb, or both.

"Mr Miller..." Her pen hovered over her notes. "We understand Ben Davies owed you a substantial amount of money. Would that be correct?"

Keith's gaze flicked up, brown eyes blinking with a nervousness that belied his indifferent slouch. His gaze passed between the detectives as though wondering which was the good and which the bad cop. "Ben had debts all over town," he said, his voice a smoker's rasp. "It's no secret. Everybody knew."

"Most people don't threaten others to get their money back," Dewi leaned in. "They don't have a reputation for making threats."

"Threats?" He laughed, the sound hollow in the quiet room. "Who told you that?" His eyes narrowed.

"We talk to people." Yvonne tapped the pen on her pad. "We hear what goes on. And when you walk around flanked by Brandon and Tony Jones, most people would take those threats seriously."

"I might have a word with people occasionally. I wouldn't call it threatening. If people owe me money, I ask them for it back. It's not illegal."

"Words are often precursors to action, though, aren't they?" Yvonne continued, her tone even but insistent. "Especially when there's drug money involved."

Miller's jaw tightened, the stubble shadowing his chin bristled like a warning. He crossed his legs under the table, stuffing his hands into his jeans pockets. "I don't do that stuff anymore. I haven't been dealing for a long time."

"Really?"

"And so what if this Ben owed me money? What about it? I didn't lay a finger on him." He shrugged. "Everyone talks tough at the pub, especially after a few beers. It means nothing. It's only a bit of banter."

"Unless someone winds up dead."

An awkward silence stretched between them.

"Do you pay them?" The DI leaned back in her chair.

He frowned. "Pay who?"

"The Jones brothers."

"What do you mean?"

"For them to back you up when demanding money with menaces?"

The muscles in Miller's rugged face stiffened. "People should pay their debts," he muttered.

"Sorry?"

"If I owed someone money, I would pay it back when I say I would."

"Meaning?"

"Meaning, maybe Ben was asking for trouble because he didn't pay his dues. It's a question of honour."

"Was the trouble he got into that night down to you?"

"No."

"You sure about that?"

"Yes."

"Where were you after closing time at The Buck, on Friday the fifth of March?"

"Home," he replied, though the quick glance away suggested otherwise. "Alone."

"Convenient..." Dewi folded his arms, eyebrows arching.

"Being alone at home doesn't make me a killer," Keith shot back, hands clenching; knuckles white.

"How did you get home?" Yvonne asked.

"I had a lift."

"From whom?"

"I can't remember."

"Brandon Jones, by any chance?"

"Could have been. I'd had a few pints... But I often get a lift or take a taxi. I don't always remember who drove at the end of a heavy night."

"Do you own a car?"

"I've got a runaround, yes."

"An SUV?"

"No, mine's a silver sports Audi."

"Did you, Brandon, and Tony Jones follow Ben Davies, Tom Howells, and Hayden Pryce up Dingle lane after they left the pub?" she asked, voice steady.

"No." Miller's response was fast. Too fast. Like a twig snapping underfoot. "I don't know what you're talking about."

The DI noted the way his eyes darted away; his fingers picking at the frayed holes in his jeans where tiny white threads lay exposed. "We have a witness who claims otherwise."

He shifted in his seat, face paling. "All right, all right." He held his palms out. "I was in Brandon's SUV, but only till we reached the bottom of Treowen Hill. They dropped me off there, and I walked home."

"Was anyone with you when you walked up the hill?"

"No, I was alone."

"What about Rob Lloyd?"

"He stayed in the car with Tony and Brandon."

"Are you sure about that?"

"Positive. You know I live up there. You've got my name and details on your paperwork." He pointed to her notepad.

"That's right..." Yvonne's eyebrow raised. "Rob lives on Treowen too, doesn't he?"

He nodded. "Yeah... Not far from me, actually."

"The rumour is he works for you?"

"People will say all sorts, usually to save their own skins."

She flicked through her papers. "Five years ago, the courts convicted you of possession with intent to supply Class B — cannabis. You served eighteen months of a two-and-a-half year sentence. Am I correct?"

"If it says so there, it must be true."

She shook her head. "You are making this harder than it needs to be."

"Yes, I did time for dealing. But I got myself straight, didn't I?"

The DI did not believe that for one moment. "Then why does the rumour mill suggest Ben Davies owed you money for cannabis supplied by you?"

He shrugged. "They probably have me mixed up with someone else, innit? Because I used to deal."

"Did anyone see you arriving home?"

"I doubt it. But you'd have to ask them."

"I understand you live in flats?"

"Yeah."

"And there are other flats above and below you?"

"Yeah."

"But you didn't see anyone on the way in?"

"I can't remember. I don't think so. Can I go now? I have a doctor's appointment."

She checked her watch. "For now..." She nodded. "But rest assured, Mr Miller. We will speak with you again."

∽

Rob Lloyd shifted uncomfortably across the table in interview room two. His lean frame shrank under Yvonne's gaze, while the overhead lighting cast shadows across his angular face.

Dewi took his time organising the paperwork.

"Let's circle back to the night of March fifth at The Buck," Yvonne began, sensing their interviewee's emotional turmoil. "Walk me through what happened after you left the pub."

He pulled at the drawstrings on his hoodie, tightening the material behind his neck. His short fair hair appeared dishevelled, as though he'd been raking his hands through it all morning. "It was just a regular night, you know?" he cleared his throat, avoiding her gaze. "Me and Keith left together. We got dropped off at the bottom of Treowen Hill."

The room fell silent. Yvonne studied his face. "Really? I thought Keith went home alone?"

"He did." Lloyd cleared his throat. "We only walked up the hill together. We live on the same estate."

"Who was driving?"

"Brandon... It was Brandon's SUV. His brother Tony was in the passenger seat, and Keith and I were in the back."

"Was anyone else with you?" She leaned forward. Blonde hair framing her face; capturing his attention for a moment.

"No," he said finally. "It was only the four of us. I often walk home from town, but that night I took the offer of a lift."

"Why?"

"Why did I take the lift?"

"Yes, why do something different that night?"

He shrugged. "I was feeling extra tired. It had been a busy week."

Yvonne noted a hesitation before he spoke. Was he afraid of the brothers? "And after being dropped off, where exactly did you go?"

"Straight home," he answered, but the word sounded brittle and uncertain.

"Directly home?" She asked, noting his change in body language.

"Uh, yeah." He fidgeted in his chair, eyes moving to the paperwork on the table.

"Rob..." The DI's tone softened. "We need to know everything that happened. It's important. Men died that night, and you may know something. I understand you may be afraid to talk, but we cannot help you if you do not tell us the truth."

His eyes flickered, as though witnessing the events of that night again; secrets clawing at his conscience.

Yvonne watched him patiently, sensing he was faltering, teetering on the brink of talking.

"Look..." He stopped himself, Adam's apple prominent as he swallowed hard.

"Take your time..." Yvonne picked up her pen. "The truth has a way of freeing us, no matter how dark the story..."

Rob met her gaze, fingers still toying with the drawstrings on his hoodie. "I told you, I went straight home."

"Alright..." Yvonne sighed. "Let's elaborate a little. We have CCTV footage that says that you didn't get out at Treowen Hill at all."

He held his breath, his hands moving to the table; gripping the edge as though the walls were closing in around him. When he exhaled, both hands went to his head, fingers tangling his hair. "Okay, okay." His gaze dropped to the table, as though to hide what was in his eyes. "I stayed in the SUV with Brandon and Tony. But only for as far as Garthowen, I swear."

Yvonne folded her arms. "Why Garthowen?"

"Then they dropped me off at the chip shop," Rob shrugged. "I was hungry, you know? I thought I'd grab some food before walking home."

"You went to the chippy?"

"Yes... I go there often on a Friday after a few pints. Nothing hits the spot like fish and chips when you've had a few. I'm not one for kebabs or pizza. I like good old British fare. Not every Friday, like, but most Fridays."

The DI made notes, allowing him time with his thoughts before continuing. "Benefits aren't much to live on, are they, Rob? It can't be easy, that precarious balancing act of appointments and job searches; sporadic benefits as sanctions for not following the instructions from your work coach. Threats looming over you like dark clouds ready to burst at the slightest misstep."

He shrugged. "They're always sanctioning me. How did you know?"

"Educated guess?" She raised a brow. "How on earth do you survive?"

"I get by."

"With a little help from your friends?" She cocked her head.

He shifted in his chair.

"How do you feed yourself?" The question was deliberate, cutting through the silence with the precision of a scalpel. "I mean, benefits only stretch so far, don't they? And when they sanction you, there is nothing coming in. Am I right?"

"I do odd jobs." He avoided her eyes, focusing instead on brushing away invisible fluff from his sleeves. "Gardening, painting, decorating… whatever people need."

"People around town suggest you're working for Miller." She leaned forward, hands on the table between them. "Is there any truth to that?"

He shook his head, a touch too vehement. "Look, I live in the flat above Keith's. We're friends, that's all."

"Are you sure about that?"

"Yes."

"So, you didn't follow Ben Davies and his friends up the lane towards Dolfor that night?"

He shook his head. "No."

"You didn't go along to help put the frighteners on him and his friends, to get him to pay Miller the money he owed?"

"No."

"You see, we have a witness who saw a vehicle, exactly like Brandon's, whose occupants were having a heated argument with Ben and his friends. Was that you?"

"No."

"You, Tony, Brandon, and Keith?"

"No."

"Putting pressure on those three lads?"

He swallowed.

"Perhaps you were there under duress? You didn't really want to be there at all, but couldn't let your friend Keith down?"

He shook his head, looking at his hands. "No."

"And, if we approach Garthowen chippy for their CCTV from that night, it will show you getting food at eleven-thirty, will it?"

He swallowed.

Yvonne exchanged glances with Dewi. "Alright, Rob. We'll be in touch."

∼

OUTSIDE, the sky threatened rain. Dark, bulbous clouds hung low over the town as the DI and Dewi walked to their unmarked car, spattering their contents onto the windscreen as Dewi fired up the engine.

The drive to Dolfor was quiet, save for the rhythmic swish of wipers across the windshield. Five miles out from Newtown, the world became a pastoral hush, permeated only by the murmuring of sheep and cattle, in stark contrast to the traffic they had left behind.

The Wright family smallholding nestled amid green fields and blossoming hawthorn hedgerows. After parking the car outside of the main gate, a barking sheepdog greeted them, providing ear-splitting accompaniment all the way to the front door. By the time Emily opened it, however, the dog was sitting on its hind, panting and dripping thick saliva as it sniffed the air.

"Hello, Emily? I'm DI Yvonne Giles, and this is DS Dewi

Hughes." The DI smiled at the young woman dressed in a tee-shirt and jogging pants.

"Please come in." Emily stepped back. "Forgive my casual appearance. I have yoga later this afternoon."

She was younger than Yvonne by a good twenty years, with an energy that seemed at odds with her quiet surroundings and the dull tick of the large Edwardian clock dominating the mantlepiece. As she showed them to armchairs in the large sitting room, she adjusted the band holding her long, dark hair in a ponytail, and sat on a covered stool near a large bay window overlooking the fields. Her eyes studied the detectives expectantly.

"Thank you for seeing us, Miss Wright," Dewi said, as they settled into two faded floral chairs. The atmosphere was homely, with pictures of the family through the ages dotted on shelving.

"Of course." Emily placed her hands in her lap, back perfectly straight. "Have you come to ask me about Ben?"

"Yes." The DI pulled out her notebook. "We understand you were Ben Davies' girlfriend?" She tilted her head, eyes soft with empathy. "We are sorry for your loss."

"Thank you." The girl's eyes glazed and darkened for a couple of seconds. "I can't believe it. It's such a shame. He was a nice guy. All three of them were good guys." She sighed.

"How long had you two been seeing each other?"

"Only a couple of months." She began cuddling a cushion she grabbed from beside her. "It was all still quite new, really."

"Did you see Ben at all on the night of March fifth?" Yvonne studied her face.

"No, I didn't see him. I only wish I could have." She sighed, shoulders dropping, a crease forming between her brows. "He texted me earlier in the evening, but he didn't say he was coming over. I wouldn't expect anyone at that hour, especially when my parents are away. I am nervous about late night visitors."

"It must be difficult," Yvonne observed, "being here alone, looking after the house and the animals."

"It is..." The girl's voice trailed off. She turned her head to stare through the window as rain splattered its panes. "But I manage. It's worse at night when it's dark. I wish I had known they were out there. Maybe I could have helped them somehow... alerted the authorities earlier. I hate to think of him and the others out there, alone. And it was so cold. I hope they didn't suffer too much."

The rain intensified, tapping an insistent rhythm against the glass as though wanting to take part in the conversation. Inside the Wright's sizeable living room, Yvonne allowed a moment of silence as respect for the dead men before her eyes locked onto the girl's. A sadness lay in those blue depths. Or, perhaps, it was the burden of knowing more than she let on.

"Emily," the DI said with gravitas, "we believe Ben and his friends intended visiting you that night. It's one of the few reasons we can think of for them heading up this way. Unless you can think of any others?"

Dewi made notes, forehead lined in concentration.

"Would he really have been coming here without telling me, though?" She frowned. "I mean, Ben knew I don't like unexpected guests, especially late at night. I told him noises out here made me nervous, giving me nightmares. Don't get me wrong, in hindsight, I wish they had turned up here all in one piece. I just don't know if this was their intended destination. But, if it was, I wish he'd told me he was coming."

"Was there any reason he might want to see you? Perhaps something urgent, or something he mentioned in passing? In one of those texts you mentioned?" She noted the tremor in Emily's long fingers, and the way her gaze darted away for a moment.

"Not that I can think of." The young woman shook her head, her voice gaining strength as she clasped her hands together. "He asked how my day was, the usual stuff. He never said he would come here that night."

"Could he have been running from someone? Did he mention owing money to anyone?"

"No, never."

"And yet their car crashed only four miles from here," Dewi interjected. "And from what we've pieced together, they were heading in this direction. There's nothing else between here and town."

Yvonne leaned in, narrowing her focus on Emily's face. "We really think Hayden was driving Ben out here to see you."

Emily pursed her lips. The wind began howling, an eerie accompaniment to the conversation as a darkening sky threatened thunder.

"Are you saying this may have been my fault?" Emily's brow furrowed, as though considering this for the first time. The fire crackled in the hearth from a downdraft in the chimney.

"Not at all. Please don't think that. No-one is assigning blame here," Yvonne reassured. "But pinpointing where they were heading, and why, could help us understand what happened to them... And why they died that night."

"Ben would do foolish things sometimes, to surprise me," Emily murmured, her gaze dropping to the floor as if she could find answers in the worn carpet. "Maybe he thought it a romantic thing to do." She sighed, as though something troubled her.

"What is it?" Dewi asked, sensing like Yvonne there was something the girl wasn't saying.

Emily shrugged. "I don't know of anything. Like I said, Ben knew I was afraid of bumps in the night. I don't think he would have wanted to scare me. I doubt he was coming here."

The DI was not convinced. Emily's expression and hunched posture suggested she was holding something back. "Perhaps there was something only you and Ben knew?" Yvonne cleared her throat. "Something you are afraid of talking to us about? Maybe to protect Ben? The full picture is still emerging, Emily. Any details you have could be the key to unlocking what happened that night."

The young woman shrugged. "I can't think of anything. I'm sorry."

"Your folks are in South Africa, is that right?" Yvonne changed the subject, her tone matter-of-fact.

"Yes, they'll be away for another fortnight," Emily's shoulders relaxed, though she was wringing her hands in her lap, a fact not lost on the detectives.

"Looking after all this on your own must be quite a responsibility." Dewi's observation was gentle, his attempt to put the young woman at ease almost paternal.

Emily nodded, her gaze drifting toward the distant fields. "It keeps me busy. The animals don't feed themselves. It gives me something else to think about instead of dwelling on... well, you know..."

"Of course," Yvonne said, shifting gears as seamlessly as the dark clouds scudding over the fields. "So, tell us about Ben. What was he like?"

"I didn't know him all that well, really. Like I said, it was all still new. But, he was funny and warm. A gentleman. He made me feel special, and wouldn't take no for an answer when he first asked me out. He was a whirlwind, and he deserved better."

"Better than what?"

"Than what happened to him."

The DI had the distinct feeling that wasn't what the girl had intended to say. She pressed her lips into a thin line. "I see." Her flint-sharp gaze locked onto Emily's. "What did his texts contain that day?"

"It was mainly small talk. He asked how my day was, how the animals were coping without my parents..." She trailed off, her attention momentarily caught by a horse neighing out in the paddock.

"Just normal banter?" Yvonne pursed her lips. "Do you still have these messages?"

"Some... I deleted most of them, unfortunately," Emily murmured, eyes avoiding Yvonne's scrutiny. "I really wish I hadn't, now."

"Why delete them?" Dewi asked.

"I wouldn't normally keep many texts on my phone, only the essential ones, like dates for an event or night out. I have one or two texts from him still on my phone. Would you like to see them?"

"That might be helpful." Yvonne nodded.

The girl left the room. It was several minutes before she returned. It left the DI uneasy.

"Sorry, I'd left my phone charging in the kitchen. Here..." She handed the device to the DI.

"Thank you." Yvonne flicked through the texts. "So you received one from him at three o'clock that afternoon?"

"Yes, that's right." She cleared her throat, shifting position on the covered stool.

"I see nothing out of the ordinary," Yvonne murmured, still scrolling.

"I told you. There was no mention of him coming here, and no mention of any trouble."

"Did you delete any sent from Ben on that day or evening?"

"No... because of what happened. I no longer had the heart to clear my phone's memory."

Yvonne handed it back to her. "Thank you. Would you say it was unusual for Ben to make plans and not follow through?"

"Ben was spontaneous, but not reckless, as far as I knew him." Emily tilted her head in thought. "It was so cold that night. Snow and ice everywhere... He knew this place was isolated. It's all open fields and long shadows up here."

"And someone could use those shadows to their advantage." The DI glanced at Dewi before turning back to Emily. "We'll let you get on. Enjoy your yoga. And, if you think of anything else, call us. Sometimes, the most important truths are the ones people don't realise they are holding onto," she said, rising from the chair. "Thank you for your help, Emily. We'll let you know if we need to speak to you again."

"Anything to help," she replied, but her smile didn't quite reach her eyes.

As the detectives stepped out of the farmhouse, the door clicked firmly shut behind them.

"Do you think she deleted texts?" Dewi asked.

"She took her time bringing the phone to us, didn't she? I get the feeling she is hiding something, but perhaps they simply had an argument that day. Maybe Ben was on his way up here to apologise. I think we should ask Callum or Dai to contact her mobile company. There were five texts in all from Ben on her phone. If it turns out he sent more, we could question her again. I don't wish to pry unnecessarily, but something doesn't sit right. She might be withholding something important."

"I agree." Dewi turned his collar up against the wind and rain.

They took advantage of a pause in the downpour to run to the car.

10

LIAM STONE

A tiny bell rang out as Callum pushed open the corner shop door in Llanidloes and walked inside, his broad shoulders covered by a long black overcoat, collar up against a chill wind that seemed unending.

He flipped open his notepad, pencil perched behind one ear; a cigarette behind the other, while a young woman eyed him from behind the counter, fascinated. "Can I help you?" she asked, cutting the string on a stack of newspapers.

"DC Callum Jones..." He held up his badge. "I'm here to talk to you about the missing backpacker, Liam Stone," he said, his tone official, but giving her a reassuring smile. "I understand he used his debit card here prior to going missing."

"Yes, he did." She nodded. "I gave the police officers who came earlier copies of our CCTV footage. I hope that was all right?"

"Yes, that is great." He pulled the pencil from behind his ear, licking the tip before asking his next question. "Exactly what did Mr Stone buy from your store?"

The shop assistant fidgeted, her fingers tracing the edge of the register.

Callum guessed she was early twenties, probably not much older than Liam Stone himself.

Her wide eyes darted to the door, then back to Callum. "He bought snacks, um... Bacon, sausages, bread, and milk, and asked for forty pounds cash back." She raised her brows as though to ask if that was enough.

"And after that?" He finished scribbling before his sharp gaze locked onto her hands, which she wrung as though squeezing the information from them.

"He left." Her fingers stilled. "I don't know where he went. People come and go all the time, and I didn't think to ask him. I just wished him a good day."

"Are you sure he said nothing more? Like mention his plans or how long he would be in the area?" he pressed, searching for anything he could take back with him.

"No, nothing, I'm afraid." She shook her head, a strand of sandy hair falling onto her pear-shaped face. "He just seemed like any other customer, and I was a little busy with stock-taking at the time."

Callum exhaled, his breath visible in the cool air of the shop. The missing camper's trail was in danger of growing as cold as the weather; the man seeming more elusive by the second.

He glanced around the shop's interior, noting the camera positioned in the corner. "Was the CCTV footage from that camera?" He pointed to it.

"Yes, I gave the officers all the hours we had from that day. Unfortunately, some of it may have been overwritten. But I think they said they had footage of him on it."

"Thanks for your time," Callum said, flipping his notepad shut.

As he stepped out of the shop, the bell above the door chimed again, as though underlining the brief, almost fruitless, encounter. That's your lot, it said. Expect nothing more.

Outside, the tiny town of Llanidloes stretched before him, a warren of streets reaching down to the river. Liam Stone was unlikely to still be around. He pulled a cigarette from the packet in his pocket, staring at it, before putting it back in the box. The longer he waited for his next smoke, the easier it would be to give them up. And he still wanted to do that, eventually.

"Let's canvas the area," Dai suggested when his dejected colleague rejoined him at the car. "Let's see if anyone else saw Stone while he was here."

"I guess it's worth a shot," Callum agreed. The two of them began plodding through streets; tapping the locals for information in the quiet Welsh town fifteen miles from Newtown.

~

Yvonne surveyed the rows of unassuming houses in Barnfields, an estate north-east of Newtown, as she and Dewi approached Dilwyn Jenkins's family home.

"Callum left a message," she told the DS after listening to voicemail. "They're knocking on doors, and going through CCTV from every shop and street corner in the Llanidloes area, looking for evidence of the missing man, Liam Stone."

"Have they found anything yet?" He asked, eyes scanning the front garden of the Jenkins's house, spying a battered Land Rover in their lean-to.

"Not yet." She sighed. "I hope it's only a matter of time... Liam has to have left traces somewhere."

Dewi rapped on the PVC door.

When it opened, Dilwyn's wife Pat appeared in the frame, her slender form diminutive as her fingers curled around the edge of the door, knuckles pale.

"Mrs Jenkins? I'm DI Giles, and this is DS Hughes. May we come in?" Yvonne's tone was polite but firm.

"Of course." Pat stepped aside, allowing them entry into the dimly lit hallway. Inside, the house appeared meticulously kept, and the DI caught a whiff of air freshener or cleaning fluids as they passed into the lounge.

"Please, call me Pat," she murmured, her gaze flitting between the detectives as she led them to a modest two-seater sofa. They settled on the pale-blue couch, while Pat plumped cushions on one of the two armchairs before perching on its edge, nowhere near the fattened cushions she had prepared, posture rigid; eyes round.

"We're investigating the deaths of three men in woods above The Dingle," Yvonne began, watching the woman's face for any flicker of emotion. "We understand your husband was out the same night those men crashed their car and wandered into the trees."

"Is my husband in trouble?" Her voice trembled, and she swallowed hard.

"We are still gathering statements from those who saw the lads, your husband being one of those." Dewi interjected. "We understand you went up there to pick him up?"

Pat hesitated, eyes darting towards the window before returning to the detectives. "Not from the Dingle… I didn't pick him up from there. I drove to Garthowen shops. He had parked the car along Plantation Lane. He was a bit the worse for wear, if you get my drift."

The DI grimaced. "We know, we saw the aftermath."

"Oh yes, the damaged cars…" Her words tumbled out,

edged with a nervous energy. She ran a hand through greying-blonde hair. "He made a bit of a mess, didn't he?"

"He did."

"He's learned his lesson, you know. I think that night's events taught him something he won't forget in a hurry."

"Would you mind telling us about that evening?" Yvonne sat back on the sofa, her gaze not leaving Pat's face.

"Um, it was like any other night, really," she faltered, the tremor in her voice belying her words. "Dilwyn was late coming home, as he often is after drinking. He loses track of time after a few pints."

"Late coming home, from where?" the DI prompted

"From The Inn, at Dolfor. He used to work on a farm out that way, and he still has several friends who drink and eat at that pub. He pops along there a couple of Fridays a month." Pat twisted her wedding ring around on her finger.

"What time did he leave the establishment?"

"It would have been closing time, around eleven that night."

"Were you surprised he took the car?"

Mrs Jenkins cleared her throat, eyes turning to the window again. "You'd have to ask him," she said.

"Of course, we will continue to speak with him directly," Yvonne nodded, "but he has difficulty remembering because of his level of intoxication that evening, so parts of his story require clarification or corroboration."

"He isn't here, at the moment," Pat interrupted, a flush creeping up her neck. "I don't feel comfortable talking about him when he isn't here."

"Was your son with you when you picked up your husband?"

"Ryan?" She swallowed.

"Yes, is he home?"

"He's at work."

"But he was there that night?"

"Yes, he was. Ryan and I picked Dilwyn up, together." Pat's voice dropped almost to a whisper, her gaze fixed on the carpet. "My husband called us from near Garthowen shops, said his car wouldn't start."

"Did he say why he was there?" Dewi asked, taking notes.

"He said he had drunk too much to continue home, and could we collect him? Other than that, he said very little. Nothing that made sense, anyway. He mumbled a lot."

"Was he injured?" Yvonne inquired, curious at Pat's obvious discomfort.

"Drunk," Pat corrected with a bitter twist of her lips. "Slurring his words, and he had sick all over his shoes... It wasn't the first time he'd gotten himself in that state, but I hope it was the last."

"Can you remember anything he said?"

"Not really..." She sucked on her bottom lip, eyes darting between the detectives, clearly uncomfortable talking to them. "He was mostly muttering to himself like he does in his sleep, when he is having a nightmare. He was really pleased to see us, told me told me he loved me and wanted a hug, but the beer breath and smell of sick from his shoes was off-putting to say the least. A lot of what he said was incoherent."

"Did he mention anything about seeing the three men? Or witnessing a vehicle crash at The Dingle?" Dewi interjected, leaning forward to better hear Dilwyn's wife. "Perhaps the next day, after he had sobered up?"

"I didn't hear him mention anything like that." Pat's breathing had sped up; the rise and fall of her chest amplified. "I think he talked nonsense, mostly. We had drunken mutterings on the night, and moaning about feeling hungover the next day. I remember he groaned a lot the morning after."

"I see... Thank you, Pat." Yvonne closed her notebook, her expression unreadable. "Would you ask Ryan to contact us, please?" She handed over a card. "Your husband is the only witness to what happened that night. Anything he said, even inebriated, could help put us on the right track in finding out exactly how those men came to be wandering in the forest in freezing temperatures."

The woman nodded, placing the card on the coffee table. "I'll let him know."

As they left the house, Yvonne mulled over Pat's demeanour, piecing together the tiny fragments of testimony they had gathered so far. But, in truth, they were not much further forward.

∼

RYAN JENKINS LOOKED OLDER than his twenty years. He sported a full beard and moustache, and thick, sandy hair. Broad-shouldered, with powerful hands, he looked like he could handle himself. That he didn't want to be there was clear from his frequent sighs and watch-checking.

Yvonne arranged her papers. "Thank you for coming in, Ryan. We hope not to keep you long. Did your mum explain why we wanted to speak with you?"

"She said something, yeah." He shrugged. "I don't know if I can add anything to what she already told you, though," his deep voice vibrated.

"I understand." She nodded. "We are building a picture of what happened on the night of the fifth of March. You will be aware that three young men, about your age, died up at The Dingle."

"Nobody murdered them, did they?" He frowned.

"No, we are not saying that. But their behaviour was odd, running up the hills and into the trees like that, especially after they had been involved in a traffic collision. Their bodies lay some distance from one another. We found that odd, too. Why were they not walking together? And their families want to know why they walked away from town, after driving a location that was nowhere near their homes. Any information we glean about that night could help give those grieving and confused families some closure. You can understand that?"

"I guess..."

Her gaze settled on his forehead, and the perspiration reflecting the light.

Dewi's eyes fixed on Ryan's hands, and the fingernails gnawed to the quick. "Was your dad in any fit state to talk to you when you picked him up that night?"

"Not really." The answer was curt, like he wished to dispense with the subject quickly and move on. He swallowed hard. "My dad could hardly stand. Kept going on about needing to get away from there."

"From Garthowen?" Yvonne frowned.

"Yeah, from Garthowen." His eyes darted between the DI and Dewi, as though attempting to work out where their questioning was going.

"Did he mention anything about a crash? Or about seeing the three men?" Her tone was patient, but firm.

"He was rambling and not making much sense. Like I said, he was drunk." He emphasised the last word, like it was a shield deflecting further inquiry.

"Ryan," Yvonne said, her voice softer. "If there's something you're not telling us, it's important you do so now. This is a serious matter."

"Look, it was late... or early, however you want to look at it. He rang us and sounded off his face." He hesitated, licking lips which were chapped like his large hands. "We found him near the shops, staggering about. Mum had to help him into her car."

"Unsteady on his feet, and unable to walk unaided because of drink?" She made notes.

"Basically.... Yeah." He shrugged. "Dad was a mess, and couldn't have walked very far without ending up in the gutter."

"And you are sure he didn't mention a crashed vehicle, or men approaching him up an embankment?"

Ryan shook his head vigorously, beads of sweat trailing down his temple. "No. I swear, he didn't mention any crash. He was too out of it to talk about anything, only mutter nonsense."

"That is exactly what your mum said." She watched him, feeling he was holding back, wondering how to peel back the layers to get to the truth. Her instincts screamed of Dilwyn Jenkins' involvement in what happened that night, but she couldn't force either him or his family to talk.

"Thank you, Ryan," she said finally. "That will be all for now."

His eyes met hers, lending a flash of something unreadable before he glanced away. "I want to help you, I do. But there's nothing else I can tell you. Dad said nothing to me about the three men or their vehicle."

. . .

OUTSIDE, Yvonne sighed. "Something's not right," she murmured, more to herself than to Dewi, who was himself deep in thought.

"I agree," he answered. "I think he and his mum are protecting his father. But, whatever they are hiding, we'll find it. We always do."

11

A TANGLED MESS

"Dilwyn Jenkins is downstairs asking for you, ma'am. He says it's urgent." Callum pulled a face. "I think he was drinking again last night. He looks hungover and smells of stale alcohol."

Yvonne looked up from her desk, taking a few moments to answer as she tore her thoughts away from the case. "He's here now?"

"According to the front desk, he walked in about five minutes ago. He's quite insistent, apparently."

"Very well." She nodded. "Let them know I'll be down in a couple of minutes, would you?"

"Will do."

"Thanks, Callum." She ran a hand through her hair, wondering what their flaky witness was going to say this time. If foul-play was involved in the Dingle deaths, Jenkins' testimony would be an essential part of the case. That did not inspire her with confidence.

. . .

DILWYN SAT, eyes flicking around the room; at least two days' worth of stubble on his chin, and a flat cap perched at an angle on his head. He exhaled loudly when she walked in, his shoulders relaxing. "For a minute, I thought you weren't coming," he accused.

She cleared her throat as the stench of metabolised alcohol hit the back of it. "What can I do for you, Mr Jenkins?"

He leaned back in his chair, glancing around the interview room, as though checking no-one else was around.

The DI placed her notepad on the table between them.

His skin appeared pale in the artificial light. "I need to amend my statement," he muttered, hands clasped together on the table. "I was mistaken about what I said before, and I want you to have the right account of that night."

Yvonne pressed her lips together, stifling a sigh. "Amend it? Are you sure? You've already changed it before." She kept her voice even, but her patience was wearing thin. Witnesses amending their statements were not unusual, but Jenkins seemed nervous and all too desperate to have the alterations completed quickly. Again. "Exactly what did you want to change?"

"It's about those boys... the night they..." He trailed off, unable to finish the sentence, gaze dropping to the table.

"What about that night?" Yvonne's voice was gentle, but her blue eyes bore into him. "What is it you want to say?"

"That SUV, the one I told you about..." He met her eyes. Sweat developing on his brow. "I said I saw a dark SUV on the road that night. But I—I didn't. I think I imagined it, because I'd had so much to drink."

The DI pursed her lips. "You know wasting police time is an offence, don't you?" She searched his face. What was he hiding? "I want you to consider this carefully, Dilwyn. You should only change your statement if the changes are the truth."

"They are," he answered, a little too quickly.

"You're certain of that?" she pressed, her stern voice a warning not to mess them about.

"Yes..." His answer was little more than a whisper as his gaze fell to the backs of his gnarled hands.

"All right, Mr Jenkins." Yvonne set her pen to a fresh page in her notebook. "Tell me what happened."

"Everything I said before was right, except for seeing a large vehicle on the road. I think I was hallucinating because of the drink, and the SUV was not really there. And as for the number of people on the road, I reckon I was seeing double. So it was probably only the three young men I saw."

"Really? Because you don't seem too sure, Dilwyn. Words like 'I think' and 'probably' are not statements of fact, are they? How can we rely on anything you are telling us?"

"Look, it's not my fault I came across all of this after I'd had a few, is it? I mean, if I'd known I was going to run into this situation, I probably wouldn't have drunk so much."

She frowned. "Well, you shouldn't have been drinking and driving, anyway? What happened with your court case?"

"It's next week."

"Next week?" She raised a brow? "Why hasn't the court dealt with you already?"

"They had to set a date for trial."

"Trial?"

"I've pleaded not-guilty."

"What?" She didn't know whether to laugh or cry. "You've put in a not-guilty plea to the drink-drive charge?"

"Yes."

"Why?"

"They have no proof..." He licked sweat from his upper lip. "They have no proof because they didn't breathalyse me or take any blood samples. I've only pleaded guilty to damaging parked vehicles."

"A guilty verdict after trial carries a harsher penalty." She shrugged. "And, Dilwyn, they will probably find you guilty... You surely know that? And you have given statements, in the case we are discussing here today, asserting you were so drunk you were hallucinating. You can't have it all your own way, Dilwyn. The court could charge you with contempt."

He frowned. "Only if they call you as a witness."

She put her head in her hands. Where did she start? "Has someone threatened you, Dilwyn?"

"What do you mean?" He frowned.

"The occupants of the SUV... Did they visit you? Ask you to keep your mouth shut?"

"No."

"Told you to be quiet, or else?"

"No." He pulled a face.

"Are you sure?"

He folded his arms. "I'm doing this under my own steam."

"What about the argument?"

"Argument?" He pulled a face.

"You said you heard the men arguing on the road. Or was that a hallucination as well?"

"No, I did hear raised voices. Maybe the three boys argued, and that is why they ran off. Maybe they were chasing each other."

"I'm interested only in the facts, Dilwyn." She sighed. "And not your speculation."

"I definitely heard raised voices," he scowled.

"Very well, Mr Jenkins. I've made a note of the amendments. Perhaps the deaths were a case of misadventure, after all..."

"Yes... That is exactly what I think." He appeared self-satisfied, puffing out his chest like he had just won a competition. "They crashed their car, became all dizzy and lost, and wandered off into the woods where they died of cold. That's it. It must be." He sat back, folding his arms, an irritating grin on his face.

BACK IN THE OFFICE, she sighed, shaking her head, mind sifting through the implications of Jenkins' retraction. The dark SUV had been a main focal point in their investigation. It matched with other information they had gleaned in the case. A potential lead, which was now virtually worthless. If a bully did herd those three young men to their deaths in the woods above The Dingle, he and his friends were now almost certain to get away with it.

"Everything okay?" Dewi asked, perching on the edge of her desk.

She leaned back in her chair, fingers rubbing the worry lines on her forehead as though smoothing them out. "Oh, Dewi," she said, her voice husky, "I think someone got to Jenkins. I suspect they threatened him into changing his account of that night." She stood, looking out of the window, her gaze focussing past the rain-smeared glass before turning to face him, expression sombre.

"I think that's quite likely," he answered. "It wouldn't be

the first time, and Tony Jones and his brother have a reputation."

"That's exactly what I'm afraid of." She tapped her pen against the edge of the desk. "But, if someone is intimidating witnesses, we are closer to the truth than we thought. This could be an attempt to steer us away from it."

"So we keep on keeping on." Dewi grinned.

"But what if we're wrong? What if it was simply a case of misadventure?"

He shrugged. "Then we won't find a culprit... But at least we will have exhausted every avenue and brought justice to the stories of those three men."

"Yes, you're right, Dewi. We'll keep on keeping on."

∽

THE DOOR creaked open and Tasha stepped into the hallway. "I'm home," she announced, kicking off her boots before joining the DI in the lounge. Perceptive eyes pooled with concern as she took in the sight of her weary wife. "Yvonne..." She closed the distance between them. "You look exhausted."

"I feel it," Yvonne confessed, her head falling onto her wife's shoulder as she hugged her tight. "I missed you." Her partner's presence was a welcome balm for Yvonne's frazzled nerves. "But you have travelled back from London. You don't need to hear my worries. You need relaxation. Why don't you run yourself a warm bath while I finish cooking dinner. We can talk when you have rested, over food. How was it in London? Did you get you get your man or woman?"

"We got him." The psychologist nodded. "He's cooling his heels on remand, pending trial."

"Fantastic." The DI hugged her again. "You see? I know how amazing you are."

Tasha grinned. "Hardly..." She tossed her jacket over the back of an armchair. "I'll have my bath after dinner. We'll get the kettle on, and you can tell me what's going on with your case." Her hands kneaded Yvonne's shoulders. "What's that I can smell? Is that lasagne? I'm starving."

"It is." She took her Tasha's coat from the armchair and hung it in the hall. "The food is nearly ready. Your timing is uncanny."

The psychologist grinned. "I do my best."

As they sat down to eat, with a mug of tea instead of their usual glass of wine, the DI brought Tasha up to date. "We have a mare of a case going on right now, and it feels like we are bashing our heads against a brick wall. And, just as we think we are breaking through, another wall appears behind. You know the three young men who were found dead in the woods?"

"I remember..."

"We're still trying to find out how they ended up where they did. And now we have a young backpacker who has disappeared without a trace in the Newtown area. We're chasing shadows, and our chief witness, the man who saw the three men on the road prior to their deaths, keeps changing his story. He would be pretty much useless as a witness in court, and it feels at the moment as though we will never get to the bottom of the events of that night."

"Oh, that's not good... But, you have been in similar situations before, and you came through. Why has your witness altered his statement? What changed?"

"He previously stated he saw another vehicle on the

road that night, after the lads crashed their car, and that he watched an altercation between that car's occupants and the three boys. But now he says he imagined the other vehicle because he was drunk and the three lads were likely arguing with each other," Yvonne sighed. "The guy is driving us crazy. And I have this nagging feeling we are being manipulated—like someone is pulling strings to keep us in the dark."

"You think someone scared your witness into changing his statement?" Tasha scratched her head. "Or maybe he's protecting someone? Fear can twist a story, but so can guilt."

The DI nodded. "I thought of that... I had been wondering if the man threatened those boys himself and scared them into the woods. But we're talking three fit young men versus a drunk. I can't imagine a scenario where he would have the upper hand like that. I mean, yes, they had been involved in a crash, but they had the physical strength and stamina to head off up a steep hill through dense woodland. That would surely be a tougher feat than standing up to a cantankerous, middle-aged drunk?"

"You would think so." Tasha nodded, eating a forkful of lasagne. "This is so good," she said, after swallowing and sipping tea from her mug.

"Either way, we're back to square one." Yvonne lifted her head, her blue eyes meeting Tasha's steady gaze. "No leads, and no confirmed motive. Only the woods, the bodies, and a lot more questions than answers."

"Then find new leads," Tasha stated with quiet conviction. "You're too good not to crack this case, Yvonne. You simply need a moment to breathe. Give yourself and your team time to see it from a different angle."

"You're probably right," Yvonne conceded. "Perhaps I

should think about something else for a few hours; let my subconscious have a go at it in the background."

"Let's walk it off together." Tasha placed her hand over the DI's on the table. "Tomorrow is Saturday. I say we go for a walk by the sea and have dinner by the harbour. What do you say? You're not alone in this, love."

Yvonne smiled. Not for the first time, she was grateful for Tasha's fresh and grounded perspective. Though the mystery of what happened in the Dingle woodlands hung over her like a thundercloud, time with Tasha had made her feel better already.

THE SEA AIR swept over the promenade with a briny briskness, scrubbing away the stale cobwebs from the week.

Yvonne and Tasha took the steep steps down to the beach, before strolling along damp sand accompanied by the rhythmic crashing of waves. They walked in silence, weaving lines of footprints and skimming the odd stone across the surf on Aberystwyth beach.

They talked about London, and reminisced about their wedding day, stopping now and then to watch passers-by or perch on the rocks. Having walked the full length of the prom to the kicking bar below Constitution Hill, they began the long stroll back to the castle perched on a rise to the left of the coast road that ran round past the pier and on towards the harbour.

As the evening tide retreated, they headed for their table at Rummers, the quaint restaurant adorned with flickering candles that cast dancing shadows across their table, leading the eyes down to the water through the main picture window. The soft glow of the candlelight relaxed the DI, who felt more at peace than she had for a while.

"You could try the mackerel," Tasha suggested, pointing to the menu with a knowing smile. "It really is exceptional here. Or at least it was the last time I had it."

Yvonne nodded, glazed eyes fixed on the golden flame wavering before her. Despite feeling better, the case that had burrowed under her skin like a relentless splinter still distracted her.

"Yvonne?" Tasha's voice broke through her reverie, gentle but firm. "If you need to, we can talk through your worries. Fresh eyes, remember?"

"Are you sure?" The DI exhaled, her mind slipping back to the present. "You deserve your downtime as much as anyone."

"Let's examine the victims' perspective," Tasha nodded, her criminal psychologist's curiosity coming to the fore. "Three strong young men run into the woods on a freezing night after crashing their car. That is abnormal behaviour, and suggests they had gotten lost or were frightened... The likelihood of being lost that close to town is slim, I would say. Wouldn't you?"

"That is what I think, yes." Yvonne nodded. "We have our eye on the men we thought may have scared them. Their ringleader had an argument with one of the fated boys earlier in the evening at their local pub. He has a reputation around town as a hard-man and frequents the gym daily. He also admits to having had a former cannabis dealer in his car that night. Rumours around town suggested Ben Davies owed money to this dealer."

"Right... Now we are getting somewhere. So what do we think? Was the argument over the owed money? Is the gym-goer the dealer's muscle man? Or did he have his own issues with Ben?" Tasha inclined her head, waiting while Yvonne thought about it.

"Could be both," she said finally, eyes narrowed in thought. "Could be the local hard man had a bone to pick with the boys, and did so flanked by his cronies. And the low-life dealer threw in his lot as a way of getting his money back. But would that result in those boys running into the woods? All three of them? I'm not sure it would have."

Tasha's fingers drummed on the table. "What about a weapon? Something serious enough to terrify men who might ordinarily have put up a fight."

"It's possible... Except the tough guy, Tony Jones, does not have a reputation for knives or the like. He likes to use his fists. His previous offences have been for assault and battery, not involving weapons."

"What about the dealer?"

"Keith Miller does not have a known history of using weapons and has no weapons convictions. We'll speak to drugs team in Brecon, see what intel they have on him."

"Good idea." Tasha leaned forward, her face orange in the candle's flickering light. "Fear can make people do crazy things. And I agree with you... I think those men were terrified."

Yvonne nodded. "And whatever they feared must have been worse than running through snow and ice in the dark, in little more than a tee-shirt, jeans, and light jacket. They would have been painfully cold as soon as they became exhausted and stopped running."

The waiter arrived with two plates of steamed mackerel, dressed with lemon and coriander, and served with boiled potatoes and peas.

The DI gave him a grateful nod. "It looks good, thank you."

"Enjoy," he replied, stepping away, a tea-towel draped over his arm.

"Tomorrow," Tasha picked up her knife and fork, "You can look at this case with fresh eyes. But for the rest of tonight, Yvonne, forget all about it." She topped up their wine glasses with a dry chardonnay. "I booked us into the bed-and-breakfast for the night. So relax and enjoy the evening."

12

A CLANDESTINE AFFAIR?

Yvonne was deep in thought, mulling over the case files strewn across her desk. Strands of straw-blonde hair had fallen loose from her bun, and bags under her eyes gave testament to the fatigue she was feeling, having worked since six o'clock that morning. She had wanted to get a head-start, but was unsure whether extended work days really helped in the long run.

Dai placed a steaming mug of tea in front of her. "You look like you could do with one of these," he said, taking a seat opposite. "I have news for you when you are ready. There's no rush." He sipped from his own mug before setting it down and waiting.

"Thanks, Dai." Yvonne looked up from her work, rubbing her face and yawning before wrapping long fingers around the warm vessel, drawing comfort from it. "What's the news?"

He eyed the dark lines under her eyes. "There are rumours going around town that Emily Wright broke off with Ben Davies before he met his end that night."

"Really?" The DI's brow furrowed. She put her cup

down. "We talked to her at the farm, and she spoke of him fondly, never once mentioning they had broken up. Why would she hide that from us?"

"Guilt, perhaps?" He leaned back in his chair. "She was probably worried you'd take a dim view of her. No-one likes to admit they hurt someone who died."

"It might explain why he and his friends were heading up to Dolfor that night. Perhaps he intended pleading for another chance."

Dai nodded. "Or maybe he was going to confront her. He may have wanted her reasons for dumping him. And instead he walked into a trap."

"Either way, she was holding out on us." The DI frowned. "Perhaps someone else was involved. Could she have been seeing someone, I wonder?" She eyed Clayton's face. "There's more, isn't there? I can tell."

"Another whisper reached my ear from one of my contacts," Dai admitted, tapping his the side of his nose. "The problem is, they don't have dates. It is all gossip and rumour. However, there were reports of Tony Jones being seen with Emily in the days after Ben's death. And he's married with twin boys aged two-and-a-half."

"Tony Jones... His name keeps surfacing, doesn't it." She picked up her pen, tapping it on her palm. "I wonder, is that the real reason Ben and his friends were arguing with Tony in The Buck that night? We need to dig deeper. What is she up to? And why hide the fact she finished with Ben. Is Emily afraid of looking bad? Or is she entangled in something more sinister?"

"Only one way to find out," Dai murmured, eyes narrowed. "Speak to her again. Pressure her into giving us the facts."

"If she'll give them up." She sighed, her gaze moving to

the window and an ominous grey sky. "We won't understand what happened to those boys until we wring the truth from those hiding it. Though I'm not sure we can blame people for withholding information. Tony Jones is a formidable character who is not afraid of throwing his weight around. It's possible he threatened people into silence."

"He certainly has a reputation." Dai nodded. "But if Emily cared for Ben at all, she will probably want to come clean. If she knows something, it will eat away at her."

Yvonne finished her tea. "Dewi and I will go see her again. It's time we got some honest answers."

~

A GREY PALL loomed over the Dolfor landscape as Yvonne and Dewi made their way along the path to the Wrights' farmhouse, accompanied by the earthy scent of rain and manure. Yvonne pulled her long coat tight against the chill while they waited for the door to open.

"Be prepared to read between the lines, Dewi," Yvonne murmured, her voice low. "What she doesn't say may be as important as what she does."

Dewi nodded. "I'll take note."

The door opened, revealing Emily's fragile silhouette as she led them into the kitchen. Seated around the oak dining table, her eyes flicked between the DI and DS.

Yvonne broke the tense silence. "Thank you for seeing us again, Emily. I know this hasn't been easy for you, and I know how busy you must be here on the family farm with your parents away. Have you heard from them at all?"

"From my mum and dad?" She raised both brows, surprised by the innocuous opening question.

"Yes," the DI confirmed. "With Ben's death, I thought

perhaps they would keep in touch... Support you."

"They have been in contact." The girl nodded, unbuttoning her cardigan at the heat emanating from a wood burner crackling in the corner. "They wanted to come home early, but I told them not to be daft. I'm a big girl. I can cope until their return."

"Are they enjoying their time?"

"They are." She nodded. "They are bringing a few gifts back they said. My mum loves ethnic art." Emily pointed at the African masks dotted on the walls. "I expect there will be a few more of those coming back with them."

Yvonne smiled. "Sounds like they could have a heavy load."

"I expect they will." The young woman placed her hands palms down on the table. Round eyes suggested she was wondering what might come next.

The DI took out her notebook, flicking through it while mentally phrasing her question. "Emily, we heard a rumour that you ended your relationship with Ben Davies prior to his death. Is that correct?"

The girl swallowed. "Really? Where did you hear that?"

"One of our officers heard it in town." Yvonne could see the cogs turning. "Is it true?"

The girl started shaking her head, but thought better of it. "Yes..." She sighed. "It's true. I was unsure of whether a relationship with him was practical, so I broke it off."

"How did he take it?" The DI tilted her head, voice soft.

"He was upset. Said he hadn't expected it."

"Did he try persuading you to rethink?"

"Not at the time... He was tight-lipped. I could see he was hurting, but he wouldn't say anything. It unnerved me a bit, actually. He just walked away from me."

"And how long was this before he died?"

"Two nights before."

"Why didn't you mention this when we came last time? Why didn't you tell us you had finished with him when we spoke to you?"

She chewed the inside of her cheek. "I thought you might think it my fault that he ran off into the frozen countryside and died. To be honest, I've been expecting the entire town to have a go at me. I mean, it happens sometimes, doesn't it? When one person breaks it off with another, the broken-hearted one does something drastic."

"Do you think Ben's death was suicide?"

"Don't you?"

"I might have considered it if he hadn't taken two others with him. I would consider that course of action to be a little more than drastic."

Emily shifted in her chair, fingers twisting a strand of hair while her eyes glazed over. "Maybe the others were looking for him when they succumbed to the cold."

"Don't you think Ben might have been coming here? A few beers, a little Dutch courage, and he may have felt an urge to visit; persuade you to stay?"

She shook her head. "I doubt that."

"Why? What makes you so sure that wouldn't be his plan?"

"Because..." She stopped herself. "I don't know. I just don't think it was."

Yvonne wondered what she had been about to say. "Every detail matters in an investigation like this, Emily. We heard something else, too."

Round eyes directed their attention at the DI once more, accompanied by a hard swallow.

"Apparently, people saw you with Tony Jones in the days after Ben's death. There are rumours of a romantic attachment between the two of you. Are they true? Is that why you broke it off with Ben?"

The young woman's mouth fell open, the question hanging in the air like a blade. "He's married," was all she said.

The DI noted there had been no denial, simply a statement of fact. "People have affairs," she said, her voice gentle.

For a moment, the girl seemed on the verge of breaking. But her lips pressed into a thin line. "Ben didn't deserve what happened to him. No-one deserves that. But it wouldn't have worked between him and I. I didn't care for him in the way he cared for me. I'd had a few drinks when I said yes to us dating. And I regretted it the very next day. But, at first, I didn't know how to break it off. I felt awful, like I'd been leading him on. But you have to believe me when I say I didn't mean to. I still feel bad about hurting him. I really do worry that he... that he wandered into the forest on purpose, and took his own life."

"Did you discuss Ben with Tony?"

"Yes, I-" Emily put a hand to her mouth, realising her gaff.

"So, you have seen Tony?"

"We didn't do anything together, only talked... honest. We both have feelings, but have never acted on them. It's all a bit of a mess, isn't it?" She sighed. "I don't know how it ended up like this."

"You can't blame yourself for Ben's death, however it occurred. If all you did was to break it off with him, you have nothing to beat yourself for. People break up with each other all the time. We none of us know exactly how the other person might respond, but we usually hope they will be all right. You mustn't feel bad. It is far better to be straight with us."

"Thank you." Emily's shoulders relaxed.

"So you told Tony you had been seeing Ben?"

"I told him I broke up with Ben, yes."

"How did Tony respond?"

She shrugged. "He asked me if I was okay."

"Did Ben know about your friendship with Tony?"

"I don't know."

"Did he mention Tony at all?"

"No..." She paused. "I heard that Ben and Tony argued that night. I hope it wasn't about me."

"Again, Emily, you are not responsible for their argument, even if it was about you."

"Was it?" she asked.

"We don't know." The DI shook her head.

The woman sighed. "There's nothing physical going on between Tony and I, I swear."

"I'm sure his wife would be grateful for that." Yvonne leaned back, exchanging glances with Dewi.

Before either detective could say anything further, the DI's phone vibrated in her pocket. She excused herself before reading the message, her brow creasing. It was from Callum. "I'm so sorry, Emily, but we have to go. We'll be in touch if we need to speak with you again," she said, rising from the table.

"What is it?" Dewi asked as they strode to the car.

"They found Liam Stone, buried in a shallow grave in the woods near The Dingle."

As they reached the gate, the sky opened up, releasing a deluge over the farm and fields beyond.

Putting the collars up on their coats, they ran back to their vehicle.

13

BACKPACKER FOUND

They drove to The Dingle as fast as the winding roads allowed; rain battering the windshield with a fury that matched Yvonne's racing thoughts. Dewi's grip on the steering wheel tightened, knuckles white against the leather, as they contemplated the news. It had confirmed their worst fears.

When they arrived at the stretch of woods near The Dingle, uniformed officers had already cordoned off the scene. Flashing blue lights illuminated the area, casting an eerie glow over the fields. The forensic team moved around in hazmat suits, painstakingly documenting every detail of the gruesome find.

They stepped out of the car, shoes sinking into the muddy ground as they followed the designated pathway to the SOCO tent covering Liam Stone's resting place. The pungent stench of decay hung heavy in the air, mingling with that of rain-soaked earth.

"Yvonne, Dewi," a SOCO officer nodded a greeting at them, his plastic suit crackling as he walked.

The rain had ceased, but the dampness lingered in the

air as Yvonne and Dewi approached the blue-and-white cordon marking the crime scene's perimeter. The sombre spectacle stood in stark contrast to the picturesque serenity of the woods, and murmurs from animals in the fields.

"Never thought I'd prefer the mortuary's smell to outdoor air," Dewi muttered, breaking shared silence as they ducked under the tape.

"I'll bet he's been here the whole time he's been missing." Yvonne grimaced. "Let's hope we haven't lost vital forensics."

They donned plastic suits, as other SOCO officers methodically sifted through the soil, documenting details of the makeshift grave. The hum of a generator mixed with the soft murmur of voices discussing findings and hypotheses.

"It's definitely Liam Stone?" Yvonne asked an officer, as the photographer put his camera away in a hard case.

"They buried his wallet and phone with him," he answered, his expression grave. "They smashed the phone, whoever killed and buried him here, and wrapped him in a tarpaulin sheet. A formal identification should take place as soon as a relative can be present. His parents have been staying at a place in Rhayader for the last week or two of the search."

"What about his camping gear? Was that with him, too?"

He shook his head, pulling the mask down from his mouth. "No tent, and no backpack. If he had them with him when he died, the killers must have taken them away, or they'll be around here somewhere. There are officers out searching; they haven't reported finding anything yet."

"So someone murdered him?" the DI asked, staring down at the muddy remains of the man in his shallow grave.

"Shot with a twelve-bore to the chest and abdomen.

Made quite a mess. The pathologist can tell you more at postmortem."

Yvonne nodded, absorbing the information as her eyes scanned the ground around. Sodden leaves, trampled grasses, and disturbed soil provided clues for the grim story of Liam's end.

"You're sure it was a shotgun wound?" she queried. "Not a knife or blunt force?"

"Definitely a twelve-bore, from what I can tell." The officer's gaze met hers. "I saw pellets in the crater in his chest when I was taking samples. It should narrow your suspects down a little."

She thought about the three other men who had met their end in the same wood. To her mind, it was too much of a coincidence. The deaths had to be linked. But, as far as she knew, Tony Jones did not have a gun licence. If he was accessing shotguns, he was doing so illegally.

Dewi crouched by the tarp, his gloved fingers lifting the waterproof material before he stood again. "His eyes were wide open. The killer must have taken him by surprise. Are you thinking what I'm thinking?" he asked Yvonne.

"That his death has to be linked to the others?"

He nodded. "Maybe he saw what happened to the lads and was killed for it?"

She pursed her lips. "Or maybe Liam was killed first, for whatever reason, and the boys witnessed it," she said, pursing her lips. "That would be enough to send them fleeing for their lives."

The DS placed his hands on his hips. "Maybe someone turned the same shotgun on them. Those men may have stumbled into a terrible situation by sheer happenstance. A freak coincidence."

Her expression grim, Yvonne turned for the exit. "The

sooner we find out what took place that night, the better. And the man with most of the answers had better start coming clean."

"Dilwyn Jenkins?" Dewi unzipped his forensic suit as they left the tent.

She nodded. "I don't believe we have ever gotten a truthful story out of him. He's a slippery weasel, Dewi. It's time we pinned that man down."

"He may be afraid, Yvonne." Dewi pulled the car keys from his jacket pocket. "He could be the only witness to what happened who is still alive. I'll bet he's terrified of telling us the truth."

"We have to find out whether Stone previously crossed paths with his killer, or simply stumbled upon a nightmare situation, finding himself on the wrong end of the barrel. We need his whereabouts from the moment he entered our area, to the time he met his end."

"Maybe someone wanted him silenced," Dewi nodded. "We'll put out a request for information during the press conference. Someone is bound to know something."

As the SOCO continued their work, The DI and DS made their way back to the car. Yvonne wanted another interview with Jenkins as soon as possible.

~

PATHOLOGIST ROGER HANSON stood over the stainless-steel table containing Liam Stone's partially decomposed remains. Hands, clad in latex gloves, moved with focussed efficiency.

The mortuary's air, sterile and heavy with the scent of disinfectant, could never quite mask the underlying smell of death. Tables gleamed under fluorescent lights and, in the corner, the relentless hum of refrigerators provided a low-level background noise.

Yvonne watched from a few feet away, unless called to see a specific detail, but her gaze missed nothing despite the headache tugging at her temples following another restless night.

"You can clearly see the damage caused by the Shotgun blast," Hanson murmured, as he examined the wound. "Decomposition has been faster in the damaged areas, as expected." He reached for a ruler, measuring the diameter of the ragged mess that had once been a chest and abdomen. "Pattern suggests he was facing his killer," he continued. "The force was... substantial. Direct hit to the heart, lungs, and stomach. Notice the stippling around the wound," he added, gesturing toward Liam Stone's chest, fingers tracing the edges of abraded skin where the discharge had left its brutal signature. "These tattoo-like marks confirm the killer fired the shot from close range."

The DI leaned in, blue eyes scrutinising the pattern. "Could this spread suggest anything about the murderer's position?"

"Yes," Hanson replied, adjusting his glasses as he continued examining the wound. "The dispersal is fairly tight. The shooter was likely within a few feet of the victim. I'd suggest maybe three or four."

Yvonne's jaw clenched. The clinical detachment of the mortuary did little to shield her from the emotional scene in her head. Her lips pressed into a tight line. Someone had aimed a shotgun at an unarmed hiker and shot him full-on at close range. A vicious, heartless crime that simply made no sense. "Can you estimate the time of death?" She asked, still mulling over the futility of the act.

"Given the results from entomology, and the state of the

remains, he likely died around the fifth or sixth of March. More specifically, I would suggest late night on the fifth or early morning of the sixth." Hanson's glasses reflected the mortuary lights as he examined the wounds.

Yvonne nodded, mentally cataloguing the information. Time was a vital thread in the investigation, and she intended pulling it tight. Her thoughts drifted to Dilwyn Jenkins. What had he really witnessed on the road that night, and why had his narrative changed so many times? Likely, he knew who the gunman was and had been told to keep his mouth shut. And, unfortunately, Jenkins had intoxication as a convenient excuse for being of little use. "Thank you, Roger," she said, scratching her head. "We are looking for a cold-blooded murderer, maybe a psychopath, who killed one man and scared three others into fleeing to their deaths in freezing cold temperatures. The date fits. That is unlikely to be a coincidence."

"I agree," Hanson nodded. "This victim showed no trace of either alcohol or substances, and there are no other signs of trauma. He didn't get into a fight with his killer. I don't believe the gunman gave him any time to react. There is no damage to the palms of his hands. He wasn't holding them out, pleading with his attacker. The blast damage to both biceps suggests his arms were by his side when he was killed."

Yvonne's gaze lingered on Liam Stone's lifeless form, thoughts oscillating between a necessary analytical detachment and a visceral need for justice. The room shrank around her as she replayed the victim's last moments in her mind. "May I see the hands?" she asked.

"Of course..." Hanson turned them over. "As you can see, no defensive wounds." He gently turned them back. "He didn't see it coming. Someone caught him completely off guard."

"Maybe the victim knew the killer?" She pursed her lips. "But Liam wasn't from this area and, as far as we know, had no friends or family here."

"Killed by a stranger." Hanson gave a slow nod. "Maybe he was simply in the wrong place at the wrong time."

She nodded. "Perhaps... Is there anything else I should know before I leave?"

Hanson considered for a moment. "I'll examine his organs, and the internal damage further, but so far as I can tell, everything points to deliberate, up-close violence dealt with a shotgun. Whoever did this wanted to be sure the man was dead."

"Thank you, Roger." Yvonne tucked a stray strand of hair behind her ear as she turned away from the table. One last look at the victim's lifeless form, and she exited the mortuary.

∽

CALLUM STRODE INTO THE ROOM. The door, swinging shut behind, startled Yvonne from her pondering on the case. He approached, expression earnest, pencil tucked behind his ear. "I've been digging into Dilwyn Jenkins's background as you asked, ma'am, and have confirmed that Jenkins does indeed hold a gun licence. He has had one for decades, ever since he worked as a farm manager out near Meifod. I'm told by uniform that he is terrified of losing it if convicted for drink-driving. Apparently, he has shot the odd dog in his time for worrying sheep, but is into clay pigeons these days."

"Really?" She frowned. "I knew it. We'll need a warrant to seize any weapons he has. If he has a shotgun, and we link it to Liam Stone's death, he stands to lose a lot more than his gun licence. No wonder he's been obfuscating like crazy. If he was involved in what happened to those four men, he'll be desperate to cover his tracks."

"Exactly," Callum nodded. "He may have gotten rid of the gun by now, but the searches of the woods did not find any weapon, so he may still have it on his premises. If Jenkins is involved, we should take every precaution for the search. The man may be a ticking time bomb."

"I'll speak to the DCI about a warrant." She stood, her expression determined, as she walked from the desk. "Get Jenkins in for an interview ASAP. I want him across that table from us, and I want answers."

14

DAWN RAID

Dawn had not yet painted the sky with pale hues before Barnfields awoke to police boots pounding the pavement. Yvonne and Dewi followed behind a phalanx of uniformed officers as they approached Dilwyn Jenkins's unassuming semi. The door yielded with barely a protest as the invading officers swung the battering ram known as the enforcer.

The house was still and dark until the men in blue shouted to the occupants, informing them of their presence.

"What do you want?" Dilwyn came out of his bedroom onto the landing, rubbing his eyes and squinting in police torchlight, hair tousled, a dressing gown draped awkwardly around him. His son, Ryan, came out of the room opposite, wearing only a pair of boxers.

Yvonne, hair tied back in a functional ponytail, pressed her lips into a tight line as she and Dewi moved up the stairs. "Mr Jenkins," she called, "we require immediate access to your gun cabinet."

He blinked in the torchlight. "What?"

"Your gun cabinet... We'd like the key, please. We have a warrant to search your property."

"What is this about?" he asked. "Can I get dressed?"

"Certainly." The DI nodded. "But we would still like that key."

He disappeared back into the bedroom, dangling it from his outstretched hand when he emerged. "Go ahead, it's empty," he said, with a smugness that bordered on defiance.

Yvonne exchanged a glance with Dewi, who took the key from Jenkins and opened the cabinet. He found nothing but shadows and dust in the metal casing.

"Where's the gun, Dilwyn?" Yvonne asked.

He shrugged. "Someone stole it a few weeks back... Ryan, and I went to a shooting competition near Bettws. Clay pigeons. We stopped for lunch at the village pub afterward, leaving the car unlocked. While we were eating, someone took our shotgun from the back of my wife's Land Rover."

"You left the gun unattended in an unsecured vehicle?" Dewi shook his head, narrowing his eyes at Jenkins. "There are strict rules around gun ownership. You should have known better. It's not an oversight one would expect from a seasoned owner."

"I hadn't heard of guns going missing before. It's quiet around here. I didn't think it would happen to me." Jenkins pulled a face. "I guess you never do until it does."

Yvonne kept her piercing gaze on him. "I'd like to ask you some questions, while officers search your home and garden."

Dilwyn flicked a glance at his wife in the bedroom. "Can we get dressed?"

She nodded. "Yes, and then I'd like you to join me downstairs."

When he joined her in the lounge, Jenkins was in trousers and a cotton shirt.

She took a seat on the sofa, waiting for two officers to finish searching the room before speaking.

Dilwyn sat in an armchair opposite.

"Who was at the competition, the day you say your shotgun went missing?" she asked, pen poised over her pad.

He reeled off all the names he could remember. They included Keith Miller and Tony Jones.

"Are you sure Jones and Miller were present?"

"They were there, and they had lunch at the same pub. We were all there together."

"Did you see them go anywhere near your vehicle?"

He shook his head. "I have to admit, after we left the Land Rover in the car park, I thought no more of it. It wasn't until we got home that we realised the gun was gone."

"Why didn't you report the theft to us? That would be standard practice, and the law."

Jenkins blinked rapidly. "Well, you see, I was scared..." He cleared his throat, nervously brushing at his thighs as though clearing crumbs or fluff, and shifting in his seat. "I was afraid of getting into trouble for not securing the weapon properly. I didn't want to lose my shooting licence over it."

"Did you try getting the gun back?" asked Dewi.

"We asked about it around town," Jenkins hesitated, avoiding their gazes. "We asked the people who had been at the shoot. But they all said they knew nothing about it."

"Have you always left the gun in the car?" Yvonne rubbed her forehead.

"Only while grabbing lunch." He frowned, evidently feeling it was a perfectly normal thing to do.

"Why not lock it inside?"

"Like I said, I didn't think we needed to. I mean, no-one casually passing would have known it was there."

Ryan, who had been standing silently by the window, nodded in agreement with his father. "We trusted the guys we were shooting with. We'd been to events with all of them before."

Yvonne exchanged glances with Dewi, her skepticism matching his. But without the weapon, they had no evidence of criminal involvement; only self-confessed negligence in not securing it.

Meanwhile, uniformed officers continued searching the house, their steps muffled by thick carpet. They worked with quiet efficiency, trained eyes scrutinising each drawer and cupboard. The air was tense with concentration, accompanied by the occasional creak of floorboards and rustle of objects being examined.

Despite a thorough search, the team found no guns and none of Liam Stone's missing items.

"There's nothing here." Dewi sighed. He stood in the centre of the hallway, gaze sweeping around one last time.

"Very well." The DI nodded, closing her notebook and placing it in her bag. She turned to Jenkins. "If it turns up again, you must tell us immediately."

As they left Barnfields, the morning sun crested the horizon, casting long shadows across streets that would soon come to life. In the early light, the hushed world seemed innocent, like nothing bad could ever happen there. Except it did.

WHEN THEY ARRIVED BACK at the station, Yvonne handed the names she had gleaned from Jenkins to Dai and Callum. "Please ask uniform to follow up on these names as soon as possible in connection with Jenkins's missing twelve-bore. All, except Tony Jones and Keith Miller," she instructed. "We'll speak to them ourselves. We need their movements on the day of the competition. Maybe they can shed some light on Jenkins' missing weapon, and the death of Liam Stone."

"Will do." Dai copied the names into his notebook.

Yvonne paced the room, hands pushed into her skirt pockets. "Jones and Miller," she murmured, more to herself than to Dewi. "They keep cropping up, don't they?"

He lifted his eyes to hers. "Either or both of them could be our killer," he answered. "But I've checked, and they don't own weapons. Neither would be eligible for a licence with their criminal records. But both frequent the local gun club. I have spoken with the venue, and they have strict rules around their guns. They always keep all weapons on the premises, and they assure me that no guns have ever gone missing. They offered for us to test their shotguns forensically, which ballistics can do, if we deem it necessary. But, honestly? I think Jenkins' missing twelve-bore is a more likely candidate."

"What if they were all involved... Jenkins, his son, and Jones and Miller?" Yvonne rubbed her temples, trying to ease a throbbing behind her eyes. "But why? What would be their motive? Is there a connection to Liam Stone other than their mutual location that night? And how does that link with the three men who crashed their car and ran away to die in the ice and snow? What in God's name went on?"

"Perhaps the boys met Miller because they wanted some of what he was selling," Dewi suggested, tilting his head.

"But, as far as we know, only Ben Davies used cannabis..." She frowned. "And we know he owed Miller money..."

"Perhaps he went up there to settle the debt? Maybe he wasn't intending pleading with Emily after all?"

The DI nodded. "Or maybe he told Miller he couldn't pay, and it went south from there."

"Until we find the gun, we do not know if it was the weapon used on Stone." Dewi perched on the edge of a desk.

"Right," she nodded. "All we know is Liam Stone died the same night. What are the chances of someone else being up there with a shotgun? I mean, it's possible, of course, but we have a known gun owner and other gun enthusiasts. All are innocent until proven guilty, but we have to start with them." She frowned. "Jenkins could very well be lying. He's changed his story so many times, it's hard to know what is real."

"True," Dewi agreed, scratching his stubbled chin. "But within his ever-changing narrative, there is probably a grain of truth. Even liars find it hard to make up the entire story. We just have to work out which bits of it are real."

"We keep digging," Yvonne nodded. "We go through everything. Associations, alibis, past offences, and known haunts. We have to find that shotgun."

∽

YVONNE LEANED back in her chair, observing Dilwyn Jenkins with a hawk-like scrutiny. Well aware he was uncomfortable. Although she would usually put witnesses at their ease, the man in front of her wasn't their usual witness. His behaviour and ever-changing story had put him on the suspect list. She had no intention of letting him off the hook.

He sat opposite, hands clasping and unclasping in his lap, gaze darting around the room like a cornered animal.

Light reflected off the sweat on his brow, though the interview room was cool.

"Mr Jenkins," Yvonne began, her voice cool and deliberate, "you've told us several versions of what happened on the night of March fifth. Understand, it's vital we have the truth. If you continue attempting to mislead us, understand that we will charge you with wasting police time and obstructing the course of justice. Do you understand?"

Dilwyn nodded, swallowing hard. "I know, I know. It's just...things got all muddled up in my head." His voice quivered. "It was the drink, see? But slowly and surely, my memories of that night have been coming back. I'm remembering more."

"So help me untangle it all..." Yvonne pursed her lips, tapping a pen on her notepad. "You told us you saw an SUV in the lane that night. Then you said you imagined it. Now, you say you saw this dark vehicle after all. Which is it, Dilwyn? Did you or did you not see it?"

"I did... I saw the dark SUV stop in the lane where the three boys were." He shifted uncomfortably in his seat. "It was a big vehicle, and it parked up on the lane above the Dingle."

"Go on," Yvonne urged, blue eyes fixed.

"Three men got out and began shouting at the boys."

"The boys being Ben Davies, Hayden Pryce, and Tom Howells?"

"Yes... I couldn't make out what was being said, but it looked heated, and involved some pushing and shoving."

"Could you describe the men who got out of the SUV?" Yvonne pressed, her tone more patient.

He shrugged. "It was dark, and the car's headlights made it difficult to see. They were in silhouette. I didn't want any trouble, so I stayed put, far enough away from what was happening. I needed a leak, see? So I wasn't in my vehicle. I was in the field above. I crouched down, because I didn't know what was happening, and I feared being robbed." He turned his face away, eyes glazed, as though witnessing the altercation again. He swallowed hard.

"What happened next?" Yvonne asked, leaning forward.

"I saw the boys take off into the woods, running like the devil himself was after them." His eyes widened as he recalled the scene. "I heard more shouts, and saw torches zigzagging through the trees, like those men from the SUV were hunting the lads down. I jumped back into my car and drove to Garthowen shops. Yes, I shouldn't have driven, but the beer had really hit me by then, and I was scared. I was terrified the men would come back. When I got to the shops, I called my wife and asked for her or Ryan to come and get me. I was proper shaken up by the whole thing."

Yvonne scoured Dilwyn's face, her own expression purposely giving nothing away. "And the backpacker Liam Stone... Did you see him? Was he there?"

Dilwyn's mouth opened, then closed. He swallowed again. A bead of sweat trickled down his temple. "He could have been one of the guys from the SUV for all I know... Or maybe he was with the three boys? I could be mistaken about numbers." He shrugged. "I don't know."

"He was shot with a twelve-bore, close to where you say you hid. And you tell me your twelve-bore is missing. That's quite a coincidence, isn't it?"

He scowled. "Just because my gun got stolen doesn't automatically imply it's the same weapon used to shoot Stone."

"Oh, I agree... I was merely noting the coincidence." Her eyes narrowed. "But you are saying you didn't see Liam at any point that night?"

"That is correct." He folded his arms, gaze dropping to the desk. "Likely he was in those woods, poor lad. I reckon he was simply in the wrong place at the wrong time, and got caught up in whatever was going down beyond the trees."

"And you have nothing more to add to this statement?"

"No, nothing."

"Thank you, Mr Jenkins." Yvonne closed her notepad. "An officer will see you out."

As they led Dilwyn away, Yvonne sat motionless, her thoughts churning. Something told her he had still not told them everything. They needed the missing shotgun.

LATER, while pacing the office, she stopped at the window, staring out as a grey drizzle blurred the world beyond its cold glass. Her mind wrestled with the inconsistencies in Dilwyn Jenkins's account. "Three different stories," she muttered. "What are you hiding, Jenkins?"

Callum interrupted her thoughts, his rugged features set in a frown. "Dewi told me Jenkins is still giving us the runaround?"

She nodded. "His latest version has men he can't identify hunting the lads through the woods with torches in the night, while he is crouching, terrified, in a field."

"It's like something out of a gothic novel." He shook his head.

"The thing is, it could be true. But with him continually changing the details, it's hard to know what to believe. And he has a missing gun. What has forensics said about Liam Stone's remains? Have they found any trace of his killer?"

He pulled a cigarette from behind his ear, tapping it restlessly on the desk. "Someone wearing gloves wrapped him in his own tarpaulin. It was a hasty burial. They barely covered him. Ballistics examined the shot removed from the victim and the impact pattern on his body. If we get the weapon, they can run tests for comparison. I believe they found foreign fibres too. They were on his outer jacket. His killer could have left them, but Stone could have also picked them up from a queue in a shop. So we can't rely on those alone. I guess we'll cross that bridge when we come to it, and when we have the other pieces lined up."

"I think Jenkins is afraid or complicit," Dai interjected. "I say we keep the pressure on him. If he was involved, he's the weak link. He'll cave eventually and tell us everything, provided we don't let him off the hook."

"Exactly," Yvonne agreed, blue eyes narrowing. "We can't afford to let that man out of our sight until we understand fully what happened."

SHE PERCHED on the edge of the desk. "I'd like you to monitor him. I want to know where he goes, who he talks to, and what he does... everything. Social media, too."

"Understood, ma'am," Callum replied, tucking the unlit cigarette in his pocket. "We'll keep him under the microscope."

"Good." Her gaze moved back to the window. "And remember, subtlety is key. The last thing we need is for him to tip Tony Jones and Keith Miller off. We are not yet sure who did what, but I agree with Callum. Jenkins is the most likely to cave to pressure, and the most likely to talk."

Dai nodded. "We'll keep a low profile."

15

THE MEN AND THE GUN

The phone rang as Dilwyn Jenkins and his wife watched TV, sat on the couch. Its shrill tone made them jump. Calls at this hour were unusual, especially on their landline. Dilwyn frowned as he crossed the lounge to take it.

"Hello?"

"Jenkins, it's Tony. Tony Jones." A clipped voice full of gravel reverberated down the line. "You've got some explaining to do."

"Jonesy..." He swallowed hard at the edgy tone in the caller's voice, and glanced at his wife, once again engrossed in the television drama, blissfully unaware of the belligerent voice on the other end of the line. Good. He didn't want her worried. He put his ear back to the phone. "Look, I don't know what you think I've done," he began.

Tony cut him off. "Cut the crap, Jenkins. You pointed the cops our way over the murder and they now think we committed it. They're sniffing around, and I don't like it."

"I didn't tell them you did anything."

"No? Well, you tell that to Keith. He's here with me."

Tony Jones's ice-cold voice sent shivers down Dilwyn's spine. And Keith Miller's reputation preceded him. His presence doubled the fear in the older man's chest.

"We need to sort this out," Tony growled. "Face to face. We saw your car up that lane. We know what you did."

Jenkins mopped his brow, buying time as he cast another look at Pat. "Not here," he said, voice shaky. "I won't have my wife involved in this mess."

"Fine," Tony snapped. "We'll meet you at the nature park."

"Give me an hour," Dilwyn replied, glad they had agreed to keep this away from his door, but worried about what they might do. "I'll text you when I arrive."

"An hour," Tony confirmed before the line went dead.

Dilwyn put down the phone, and turned to see his son, Ryan, who had caught the tail end of the conversation. Raised eyebrows demanded knowledge of what was said.

Jenkins flicked his head towards the door to the hall.

Once there, he pulled it shut behind them. "Pack the car," he instructed, his voice low but shaking with adrenaline.

"What's going on?" Ryan frowned. "Who was it?"

"Jones and Miller," Dilwyn snarled. "It's time we faced those bastards head-on."

∼

IT WAS NOT QUITE ten o'clock; the country lane cold and dark as they headed towards the nature park in Llanllwchaiarn, stopping only when they saw the orange glow of the lamp outside of the small church.

They left their vehicle in a lay-by flanked by trees whose gnarled silhouettes increased the feeling of foreboding.

Dilwyn's heart thumped in his chest as he turned off the headlights on his wife's Land Rover.

Ryan sat, silent and tense, beside him. Neither spoke until they exited the car.

"Remember, son," Dilwyn said, voice raised against the hum of the engine, "leave the talking to me."

Ryan nodded, pulling a bag from the back seat and throwing it over his shoulder. "They better not mess with us," he growled. "They've got it coming."

"Hush now," his father directed, taking out his mobile. "I'll send Jones a text, find out where they are. They better not have brought us out here for nothing." He tapped the keypad on his mobile for several seconds.

Ryan looked around while listening out for the sound of footsteps, the oppressive isolation a reminder of their vulnerability. Tony Jones was a known hard-man who hit first and asked questions later. And Keith Miller, though not as physically imposing, was arguably more dangerous with his money and network of shady connections. They heard the lapping of a nearby stream. Jenkins checked his watch.

A pair of headlights pierced the lane, growing brighter as the growling vehicle approached. Dilwyn dropped his mobile into his jacket pocket and clenched his fists.

Ryan shifted the bag on his shoulder, steeling himself for what might come next.

"Take it easy," Dilwyn murmured, as much to himself as to his son.

The approaching vehicle slowed to a stop, engine idling like a predator poised, watching its prey.

Finally it fell silent, and the menacing figures of Tony and Keith emerged, even larger in the pale wash of their car's headlights.

"Well, we're here... Like you asked." Dilwyn took a step

forward, followed by his son. They stood shoulder to shoulder; an unspoken gesture which said. 'You take on one, you take on both.'

Gravel crunched underfoot as the men approached.

"I didn't think you'd have the balls." Tony's lip curled with disdain.

"Yeah, well, you got that wrong..." Dilwyn straightened his back, chest pushed forward. "It's not our fault the police were looking for you."

"No?" Jones stepped forward. "How did they know we were up there, eh? The rumour round town is that you were there that night. Cowering in the field like the loser you are. Maybe you killed that backpacker, eh? Maybe you need to confess to the boys in blue; get them off our backs."

Ryan brushed shoulders with his father, knuckles gleaming white where he held the straps of his canvas bag.

"Seems you brought an insurance policy," Keith nodded towards the younger Jenkins. "The boy looks like he can handle himself," he sneered.

"I can." Ryan took the bag down from his shoulder, eyes fixed on the two men in front.

"Call it a necessary precaution," Dilwyn returned.

"I'm not afraid of you... Either of you." Jones began rolling his sleeves up as he approached father and son.

Ryan unzipped the holdall, pulling out the twelve bore it concealed. He held it up, tossing the bag to the ground.

Tony and Keith stopped in their tracks, a flicker of uncertainty in their eyes as Jones clenched his fists.

"I tell you what..." Ryan flicked the gun toward the upper lane. "Why don't you two start walking?"

16

THE TRUTH AND THE HORROR

The lane above The Dingle lay still and blanketed in darkness. The only sound was the distant murmur of occasional traffic. It penetrated the gap at the top of a window opened to reduce condensation. Dilwyn Jenkins' head lolled against the driver's door, his breathing deep and rhythmic in the aftermath of a drinking session that had lasted longer than intended.

A sudden scrabbling jolted him from slumber. Heart pounding against his ribs, he squinted into the blackness where he could barely make out three figures clambering up the bank towards him out of the foliage, their movements clumsy and erratic.

Irrational fear gripped a mind clouded by alcohol. They were coming at him... Robbers or carjackers were about to get him.

He tapped frantically into his mobile. "Ryan," he slurred, "I need help. I've got trouble."

WITHIN MINUTES, Ryan emerged from the lounge, lips pressed into a grim line. He had seen his father like this before, drunk and paranoid, but something in his voice made the younger Jenkins *feel his dad was genuinely afraid this time. He listened for his mother, but only silence greeted him. Her sleeping tablet had effectively knocked her out.*

He ran up onto the landing, took the shotgun from its cabinet, and loaded it with two shells before taking the stairs back down, two at a time. Grabbing a set of keys from a hook in the hall, he left through the front door, running the length of the garden, before hefting the gun into a canvas bag in the back of his mother's Land Rover.

Firing the engine into life, he tore down the lane, speed bumps throwing him this way and that as he accelerated into the night.

DILWYN JENKINS CROUCHED *behind the hedge, eyes still on the road as a dark SUV pulled up in the lane where the three lads had stopped to catch their breath. It came to a halt mere yards from where they stood.*

Tony Jones jumped out, temper flaring.

Jenkins couldn't know that Jones had spent the last couple of hours mulling over the argument at the pub, or that he had simmered with aggression until he and his friends could follow Hayden Pryce's car out of town and onto the country lane heading for Dolfor, watching incredulously as their targets sped up, taking the corner so crazy fast they left the road. Or that they had kept their distance at first, not knowing if the three men would make it out of the car alive. Except they did.

He couldn't make out what was being said, but he saw Jones push one of the men onto his backside. "Watch your mouths!" he barked at them.

The SUV's headlights silhouetted the younger men's faces. Their retorts appeared sharp, laden with youthful bravado, but the underlying fear was palpable.

"Let's go," Tony finally said to his friends, satisfied he had put

the fear of God into the boys. With a last glare that promised retribution were they to cross him again, he turned on his heel, motioning for Brandon, Keith Miller, and Rob Lloyd to follow. They climbed into the car and drove away, leaving behind a trail of exhaust fumes and their final threats hanging in the air.

THE LAND ROVER'S headlights cut through the darkness, throwing stark, elongated shadows across the tarmac as Ryan neared the spot where his father waited. His grip tightened around the steering wheel. Though still only twenty years old, he was big enough and prepared enough to protect his family, no matter the cost.

His father's phone call, frantic and disjointed, rang in his head. One thing was clear: danger lurked on that lonely country road. As his mind imagined what he might encounter, sweat beaded on his forehead, and the knuckles on his hands turned white.

Having little knowledge of the events that occurred only moments earlier, he pulled over and grabbed the holdall from the back seat, taking from it the family twelve-bore.

HIDDEN BEHIND THE RUSTED GATE, where he had taken an urgent leak, Dilwyn's breath fogged the chill night air as he pulled up his trouser zip and crouched in damp grass, eyes fixed on the lane, where the boys brushed themselves down after their encounter.

A thin sliver of moon peeked from behind the clouds as snow began falling again. It made distorted shadows of the men. Only muffled voices reached his ears. Was an attack being planned? To his alcohol-addled mind, it was. He squinted, trying to hear what they were saying, the silhouettes moving back and forth on the road.

"Stay away," he muttered under his breath. *With unsteady hands, he fumbled with his keys, the metal clinking against the gate as he made for the dubious sanctuary of his car. He slipped inside and locked the doors, the gate left open.*

He heard the pounding of feet on the road, followed by a frantic banging on his window.

"Please, can you help us?" they pleaded, faces pale smudges in the dim moonlight. "We need to get back to town." They pulled on his door handles. "Let us in..."

Dilwyn Sank down into his driver's seat, placing his hands over his ears. Below, he saw the fast approach of headlights and heard the screech of brakes.

"Back off!" Ryan's voice was like steel as he emerged from the Land Rover, engine left running; lights on full beam; shotgun pointed directly at the three men. "Get away from my dad's car." He flicked his gun. "Move."

The lads recoiled, putting up their hands, their plea turning to terror at the sight of the weapon. They blinked in the headlights.

"Get moving, and keep going," Ryan ordered, still believing the men had been trying to rob his father.

A rustle to his right; a movement in the corner of his eye, and Ryan's pulse spiked; his father's warning of 'six robbers' on the road flashed through his head. Without waiting, he pivoted, swinging the shotgun toward the noise and the dark figure he saw there. His finger tensed around the trigger as instinct overrode reason.

"Ryan!" Dilwyn's shout tore through the noise from the still-idling engine of the Land Rover, too late to snatch back the thunderous crack that ripped the latecomer's chest apart.

Liam Stone staggered into the open, his bewildered expression illuminated briefly before he crumpled to the ground, his wild camping adventure cut tragically short by a stray shot born of panic.

. . .

"FOR CHRIST'S SAKE, RUN!" screamed Hayden Pryce to the others, survival instinct kicking in. In a blur of motion and adrenaline-fuelled fear, Ben, Tom, and Hayden disappeared up the lane and into the woods, their flight fuelled by the horror witnessed on the road.

Ryan stood frozen, the acrid smell of gunpowder mingling with the iron tang of blood. His gaze locked onto Liam's fallen form, the enormity of what he had done bearing down on him with the weight of the night sky. The father's voice, distant and fractured, filtered through the haze of shock, words unintelligible, drowned out by the pounding in his son's ears and the stark horror lying on the earth in front of him.

∽

DILWYN'S HANDS trembled as he yanked the tarpaulin from its anchor on the hill at the edge of the wood, his breath coming in brief gasps that clouded the air. The night's events had sobered him considerably.

Ryan stood over Liam's body, shotgun hanging limp at his side, eyes wide and unseeing. The silence was oppressive, broken only by the occasional hoot of an owl.

His father shoved gloves into his son's hands, forcing him back to the present. "Put these on," he hissed, jolting Ryan from his trance. "We can't leave prints."

The younger Jenkins complied mechanically, pulling on the leather gardening gloves with trembling hands. His father's instruction sounded distant, muffled by the blood pulsating in his ears.

They worked as fast as they could, rolling Liam into his own tarpaulin, a makeshift shroud for the grave they were still to dig.

The ground was stubborn, resisting their efforts to claw at it with a trowel from the van and their own gloved hands, snatching at the earth and dead leaves in desperation. Every strike of the implement seemed to echo through the valley, increasing their fear of discovery.

"It's not deep enough," Dilwyn muttered, brow furrowed. He cast furtive glances behind as though expecting onlookers to emerge from the trees.

"I can't do any more," Ryan threw up his hands. "I'm done."

"A bit more, son... Just a bit more..."

Sweat mixed with grime and blood spatter on Ryan's face. He was numb but for the urge to conceal, to hide away the evidence of his actions. The hole they created was shallow, a paltry effort, barely able to conceal the freshly wrapped body, but time was a luxury they didn't have. Dawn was mere hours away.

They rolled Liam's shrouded form into the dent they had created. The dead leaves, debris, and snow they covered it with was the final, damning punctuation.

Dilwyn took a moment to look at the snowy mound of leaf mould and detritus. "Let's stamp it down and cover it with more snow," he suggested, stepping onto it with muddied boots.

Their grim task done, the older Jenkins cast his gaze around the field to the edge of the wood, and the items still needing to be dealt with. "Clear the camp," he ordered, his voice hoarse. "Everything goes. We leave nothing behind."

They trudged to where the dead man's tent lay among the trees. It was a small setup, a solitary man's escape from the world. A tent, sleeping bag, and a rucksack with some personal items. They gathered the lot, stuffing it in the back of the Land Rover.

"Where do we take it?" Ryan turned wide eyes to his father.

"Anywhere. Everywhere." Dilwyn shrugged, his gaze fixed on the back of their vehicle. "Bins around the estates. Make sure no

one's watching. But first, I'd better drive my car down to Garthowen. We can't leave it here."

When the younger Jenkins picked his father up from shops on the estate, the older man was groaning, rubbing his forehead.

"What's the matter?" Ryan frowned. "Don't fall apart now."

"I scraped some bloody cars when I parked up. Let's go. Let's get out of here, I can't think straight."

Their drive back was a blur of streetlights and adrenaline. They took the long route round, coming into the town from the South. At each stop, they disposed of another piece of Liam's world into a rubbish bin, careful to avoid any cameras where they could.

As the first light of dawn crept over the horizon, they were home, hoping they had hidden the evidence of their festering secret well enough from eyes and the fledgling daylight.

~

TONY JONES'S face was white in the lamplight as Dilwyn and Ryan marched him and Keith Miller at gunpoint across the dewy grass of the field next to the stream.

Ryan Jenkins, holding the shotgun, directed them on. Dilwyn, his jaw set, eyes narrowed, walked behind his son, emboldened by the lad's confidence. The expanding darkness stretched around them, providing a convenient cloak for their intentions.

"Keep walking," Ryan's voice was a growl, barely above a whisper, but its edge left no room for argument.

EACH MAN'S heart thumped for a different reason. The hunters had become the hunted. The occasional rustle of wildlife or the distant hoot of an owl were the only things to break the tension.

"Where are you taking us?" Tony asked, stopping dead. "I'm not taking another step."

"Just as well... That's far enough," Ryan replied tersely, himself coming to a halt.

Keith cast a sidelong glance at Tony, seeking reassurance now the lights and safety had receded.

"Should've known you'd be the type to bring a gun to a chat," Jones spat the words at Dilwyn. "Not man enough on your own, eh?"

"Enough talk." Ryan fixed his gaze on the blackness in front. "We're here."

They stood at the edge of a sloping bank, the ground uneven beneath their feet. Ryan adjusted his hold on the shotgun, ensuring it was visible to their dark-adapted gaze. "Turn around," he instructed, motioning with the barrel. "Face away from us."

"Now listen here—" Tony held his hands up to protest.

Ryan shouldered the shotgun, aiming it at Jones's chest. "I said face away."

17

NOWHERE TO RUN

The shrill ring of her telephone woke Yvonne from sleep. Bolting upright, she yawned, scratching her head through hair that had splayed across the pillow only moments before.

She had gone to bed earlier than usual to catch up on much-needed sleep. The clock's luminous hands told her it was almost ten-thirty. She had slept for little more than an hour. The unexpected call had to be an emergency or bad news.

"Yvonne," Callum was on the other end. She heard him blow cigarette smoke into the air before continuing. "A foot patrol reported seeing Jenkins' Land Rover bolting from Barnfields towards Llanllwchaiarn about twenty minutes ago."

She blinked, leaning forward to better concentrate on what her DC was saying. "Why? What's up?" She asked, her voice husky as she was still coming round from slumber. "Was he in a hurry?"

"I've been liaising with the control room and CCTV operators," Callum continued, his tone grave. "He headed up the Old Canal Road to the nature reserve. But the reason for my call is that Keith Miller's car tailed him all the way, only minutes behind. His car is also at the reserve."

"The nature park? What could they be up to there at this time of night? And you are sure Miller was tailing Jenkins?"

"He was well back, but kept the same distance behind for the entire way. It definitely looked like he was following him."

Her stomach clenched as potential ramifications dawned. "My God, Callum, Jenkins may be in danger. Miller may have the stolen shotgun with him. We might have another murder on the outskirts of town. If Miller and Jones killed Liam, and caused the deaths of the other three, they may try to take out the only potential witness to their actions that night."

"Exactly and, at this hour, there can be nothing good going on up there."

She could hear Callum clicking his lighter open and shut. "And we know for definite that Miller was following Jenkins?"

"We can't know for sure, but he took the same lane and parked not far behind his vehicle. That's all I can tell you."

Yvonne swung her legs out of bed. "Can you meet me there?" She asked, shuddering as the cool air chilled her back.

"About to jump in the car now," he replied. "I can be there in about twenty minutes."

"Good." She stood, reaching for her clothes. "Don't go up the lane until I get there. I'll phone the DCI and ask if he can organise an armed response team while I head out that way."

"Right," Callum agreed. "I'll meet you at the church in Llanllwchaiarn."

"Be careful," she said. "We don't know what is going on. Let's hope it is nothing, but I agree... At this hour, it can't be anything good. I don't want you taking any chances."

"Right oh," he replied as she ended the call.

The DI switched on the light, squinting in the glare as she grabbed her clothes and dressed as fast as she could, almost falling over as she pulled on her shoes while standing.

She sat back down on the bed to phone the DCI.

"Hello?"

She could hear his TV in the background. "Sir, it's Yvonne," she said, her voice urgent. "We may have a situation at the nature park in Newtown. Dilwyn Jenkins' Land Rover was seen leaving Barnfields and heading towards Llanllwchaiarn. Keith Miller's car was spotted tailing him a short while after."

Llewelyn sounded more alert than she felt. "What do you need?"

"Armed response and ambulances on standby," she answered. "There's a chance Miller has the missing shotgun. I'm heading out there with Callum."

"Yvonne, listen to me." Llewelyn's voice deepened. "Do not enter the reserve until backup arrives. You could walk into anything. We can't afford more casualties."

"Understood." She checked her watch. "I've got to go... We'll take every precaution."

"Good. I'll be there as soon as I can, but it won't be less than half an hour."

She heard him yawning and scratching his head. "Half an hour," she agreed.

"Be careful, Yvonne." Llewelyn hung up.

"Always," she said aloud, though he had gone.

With the call ended, she stood alone in the stillness of

her home, wishing Tasha was there. But she had returned to London to wrap things up for the Met's case. With a sigh, the DI left the bedroom and ran downstairs.

Flicking on the lights, she grabbed her heavy woollen coat, slipping it over the functional blouse and trousers she had donned in haste. It could take a while, and a frost was already developing. Lifting her bag and keys on the way out, she paused at the threshold, casting a fleeting glance at the photo on the mantelpiece. In a few days, her wife would be home. Everything would be all right.

A gust of cold air greeted her on the way to the car, carrying with it the earthy scent of the night and distant wood-smoke. Winter was reluctant to lose its icy grip over the world as the moon shone from a star-spattered sky. In the night's quiet, only the crunch of her boots on the tarmac punctuated the silence as she unlocked the car and threw her bag onto the passenger seat.

As she approached the tiny church in Llanllwchaiarn, the area was quiet and dark save for occasional streetlights, and the faint orange glow from the curtained windows in nearby houses. Her thoughts turned to Miller and Jenkins. Were they predator and prey? Or in cahoots? Whatever the case, both of them made her uneasy. She hoped Callum was keeping a low profile until her arrival.

~

Tony and Keith turned their backs as directed by Ryan Jenkins, staring at the tree-line. Above them, the clouds had dispersed, allowing a view of the stars as they shivered, waiting for whatever came next.

"So, what was it you wanted to say to me?" Dilwyn

Jenkins pushed his hands into his pockets. "Not so much the hard-man now, eh, Tony?"

Jones' body tensed, his neck and face heating from a mixture of fear and anger.

"You're gonna regret this," Keith hissed. "We know people. You won't be able to so much as piss in this town again."

"Quiet," Ryan commanded, hitting Miller in the back with the butt of his gun before shouldering it once more, muzzle aimed at him and Jones; finger resting on the trigger.

"Look, you don't have to do this..." Jones' voice cracked. "We only wanted to talk. The police have been asking people about us, and about a stolen gun. They want to know what happened up at The Dingle. Apparently, someone murdered a man with a shotgun the night Davies and them died. They think we did it. Why would they think that? It didn't take us long to work out who pointed the finger in our direction. But why? Why would you give them our names? There was only one reason I could think of." Tony swallowed. "It was you, wasn't it? It was you who killed that hiker. I saw your car that night. I wondered what you were doing up there-"

"Shut it!" Ryan swung a vicious kick at Jones' backside, leaving mud caked on the bottom of his jacket. "What happened up there is none of your business."

"Nobody needs to know what happened." Tony swallowed, his voice strained. "We won't say anything-"

"You don't know anything." Dilwyn snorted.

"Come on, let us go." Miller shifted the weight between his feet. "We'll keep our noses out of whatever it is you've been up to. It's none of our business, anyway. We didn't want the cops poking around us, that's all. Let us go, and we'll say no more about it."

"Too late for that..." Dilwyn exchanged glances with his son.

Two clicks resonated as Ryan pulled back both hammers on the gun, his feet in a fighting stance, posture solid, aim steady.

His father sniggered at their captives. "The hard-men of Newtown, and look at them now... I should photograph this... Send it to all the people you've picked on over the years. You don't look so scary now."

18

DRAMA IN THE CLEARING

Yvonne and Callum made their way along a path flanked by trees, accompanied by the sound of lapping water. They navigated using broken moonlight, not wanting to give away their presence with torches.

"I hear voices," Callum whispered, holding his hand up to halt the DI as she came up behind.

"Keep low," she whispered, crouching where they were, eyes alert for signs of movement. She turned up her radio to better hear the chatter coming through her earpiece. Armed officers were on their way from South Powys. Good. She returned the volume to a low setting.

As they edged closer, the voices became clearer. It sounded like Tony Jones was pleading to be let go.

The DI spotted Dilwyn and Ryan Jenkins, their postures rigid with hostility. The long barrel of a gun glinted in the moonlight as the younger Jenkins pointed it at Jones and Miller. Jones had his hands up. "Come on, mate... You know us. We will not say a word to anyone."

Yvonne's heart hammered against her ribs. "It's Jenkins

with the gun. They lied to us about the theft." She texted the DCI, confirming a need for the armed officers to arrive as soon as possible; that weapons were involved and could go off at any moment. She could almost taste the tension radiating from Callum beside her, his jaw set firm; gaze fixed on the dangerous situation in the clearing.

"They haven't spotted us," he whispered. "I could try approaching from behind..."

"We can't take that chance," Yvonne replied, her hand on his arm. "If you creep up on him, the gun could go off."

"Where the bloody hell is the ARV?" Callum checked his watch. "They should be here."

"They are on their way," she reassured him. "They are about fifteen minutes out."

They heard the younger Jenkins cock both hammers back on the gun.

Yvonne stood silhouetted by the moon. "Police! Drop your weapon!" she commanded, voice cutting through the stillness like a blade. "We have you surrounded."

The declaration hung in the air. It was a gamble, but she had felt there was no other choice. Her heart smashed against her ribs as she hoped her kevlar vest would hold up, should the worst happen. Backup might not arrive in time to save her if Jenkins were to shoot.

Ryan's head spun round, the gun still on his intended victims.

"Put the weapon down," Yvonne persisted, her voice calm despite the blood clamouring in her ears. "This doesn't have to end badly, Ryan. I don't know what is going on here, but you can still walk away from this."

She held her breath, waiting for his response. She could see his wide eyes in a face paled by moonlight. His movement jerky, he flicked the gun from his captives to Yvonne and back several times.

The DI took a step forward.

Ryan held the gun higher, still on his victims, but his head flicked between them and Yvonne as she eyed the barrel of the weapon. Her blouse felt hot on her back as it clung to dampening skin. She was glad of Callum's presence as he came up to flank her, but held out a hand, signalling for him to hold tight. There was no sense in them both getting hurt.

"Stay where you are." Ryan's serrated voice rasped as he waved the gun. "I mean it... Don't come any closer."

Keith Miller held his hands high, gaze not leaving the weapon.

Tony Jones's eyes flitted from his captors to Yvonne, breath coming in ragged gasps as his tense body poised for action. In a desperate, fleeting movement, he lunged for the weapon, primal instincts kicking in.

"No!" Yvonne held her hands out, as though they might stop what was about to happen.

With brutal speed, Ryan swung the butt of his twelve-bore into Jones's face, accompanied by a sickening thud. The stocky man staggered sideways, a guttural cry ripping from his throat as he cradled an eye, probably already swelling shut.

"Put the gun down," Yvonne ordered, outstretched hands shaking. One wrong move, and Jones, Miller, or herself could be dead.

"Back off..." Ryan's voice was hoarse, his movements erratic as he gestured wildly with the gun, bringing it back to Jones and Miller. "I swear, I'll shoot."

"Ryan, think about what you're doing. This isn't the way to

deal with any problems. The gun won't solve anything. This town has already lost four young lives. Please don't increase that tally. We can talk this through. More armed officers will be here at any moment. I don't want to see you shot. I don't want to see anyone else hurt here. Please... Put the gun down."

There followed a pause, a momentary hush where the ragged breath of men pushed to their limits could be seen and heard. An owl hooted in the distance.

The DI took advantage of the lull, edging closer, every sense heightened, her mind hunting for ways to deescalate the situation. "Put the gun down, Ryan," she repeated, keeping her voice as steady as she could. "Let's talk this through. No one else has to get hurt."

Ryan was visibly shaking, but the gun remained on Jones and Miller.

Off to her right and behind, the sound of boots on grass, and men shifting through the trees, dead leaves crunching under their weight. Emerging from the shadows, figures clad in tactical gear, their movements precise and coordinated.

Weapons drawn, they signalled to one another with practiced ease, each gesture a wordless command in the night's tense silence.

"Police! Drop your weapon and put your hands where we can see them!" An authoritative male voice filled the air, shattering the brittle calm that had settled over the scene.

Ryan Jenkins' eyes darted toward the advancing officers, his grip on the gun wavering for the first time. Laser lights danced on his chest as a powerful torch beam shone in his face, bouncing off a sweat-soaked brow. "Stay back!" He shouted, defiant even as fear cracked his voice.

"Drop it now. This is your final warning." The officer called again in a voice that meant business. Other members of the team echoed his command as they positioned themselves with deliberate care, fanning out to encircle the clearing, the net of justice closing in.

Yvonne stayed with Callum as they watched the armed team settle into position.

"Please, Ryan," she whispered, willing him to comply with the team's orders. "It's over…"

Father and son had nowhere to go, caught in the crosshairs of multiple guns.

The younger Jenkins turned the shotgun on himself, fighting with the barrel to position it under his chin, arm at full stretch, thumb on the trigger. The gesture froze the blood in Yvonne's veins.

"Ryan, don't do this," she called, taking a step forward, hands raised to placate him.

The armed men held their position, waiting and watching for the order to end the stand-off.

The DI continued. "Think about what you're doing. This isn't what you want. I don't know how you ended up in this situation, but we can talk about this. You can tell us how and why you ended up here. Think about your mum. She wouldn't want this. Your death would kill her, too."

Ryan's wild eyes locked onto hers. It was clear he didn't know what to do. "I've got nothing left." The words shook his body, like they came from some cavernous hole inside him, the steel mouth of the gun against his throat.

Yvonne inched closer, each step measured, reminding herself occasionally to breathe. "You have choices, Ryan. Let us help you make the right one." Her tone was soft despite the urgency, a lifeline thrown to a drowning man.

"It's over, son. I shouldn't have brought you here, and I should never have called you out that night at The Dingle. This is all my fault. Please don't do this," Dilwyn Jenkins's voice choked. "I can't lose you. We'll see this through together." He placed a hand on Ryan's arm.

For a moment, everything stilled.

The DI broke the silence. "Remember who you are, Ryan. You cannot change how you got here, but you can change what happens next."

The gun barrel dropped several inches.

"Let the gun go, Ryan. It's time to step back from the edge." Her gaze flicked to the armed officers, whose weapons were still on him.

A shudder ran through the younger Jenkins' frame, as he lowered the gun to his side, muzzle hitting the floor. As the weapon fell on soft earth, Ryan's shoulders slumped in surrender.

Relief flooded the DI as the armed officers raced to his position. They secured him with swift efficiency while paramedics, unnoticed by Yvonne until now, ran forward to check over the four men in the clearing.

~

THE SKY HAD MOSTLY CLEARED, allowing the moon full freedom to bathe the park with reflected light. Shadows from the trees stretched out like bars of a cage on the grass. A chill breeze caught Yvonne's coat. She buttoned it shut, lifting the collar to protect her neck as she approached the two figures standing stiff and handcuffed under the scrutiny of flashlights. Callum arrested the duo on suspicion of murder, along with multiple other serious charges.

Dilwyn, his head bowed, sighed in resignation while his son, Ryan, stared straight ahead, eyes wide and skin grey as he shrunk into himself. Both men's shoulders were slack and slumped.

The older Jenkins looked up as she approached, opening his mouth, voice crackling with emotion. "I never meant for any of this to happen. I don't know how we got here. It's all one big mess…"

Yvonne pursed her lips, eyeing the defeated man. "You understand you are under caution? That anything you say can be used in evidence?" She was confident Callum would have made this clear during the arrest, but the reminder was important, as Dilwyn clearly wanted to talk.

His son remained tight-lipped.

"I shouldn't have drunk and drove that night," Dilwyn continued, the confession spilling out in phases, like projectile vomit. "I saw those three lads coming out of the bushes at me, and I panicked. It looked like they were going to mug me or take my car. You hear stories like that these days. I read it all wrong. It was me who got Ryan involved. He should have been home, getting ready for bed after a long shift at work, but I scared him down the phone. All he wanted was to protect me. He told those boys to hop it, and they ran off into the woods. If they had been sober, they might have acted differently, too… just as I would have."

"They ran because they saw your son shoot Liam Stone dead." The DI flicked her gaze to the younger Jenkins and back.

"I know what you're thinking, but you don't understand… We didn't know who he was. Liam came… He came out of nowhere. He startled us both, and Ryan panicked. He didn't mean to shoot. It was fear, pure fear and adrenaline. We didn't think those boys would carry on running. We thought they'd hide amongst the trees, and maybe come out later."

"You didn't chase them? Make sure they wouldn't get the chance to talk?"

Jenkins hung his head.

"You told me in an interview you saw torch lights amongst the trees after the boys ran, didn't you? But it was you and your son, wasn't it? It was both of you taking torches into the trees to look for them. You wanted to be sure they wouldn't talk."

"We looked... But we didn't find them, I swear... They had disappeared amongst the trees. They must have been running like the devil. It's surprising they made it to where they died, considering their injuries and intoxication. But we didn't find them. We gave up, and we had a mess to sort..." He stopped himself.

"You had a mess to sort because you shot a man dead, and he was still lying there in a pool of his own blood, where you'd left him to go off in search of the witnesses. Why didn't you call the emergency services? You could have told them the circumstances... that you shot someone out of fear. You could have given Liam a chance of survival."

"He'd gone... We could see he had, couldn't we?" He turned to his son.

Ryan was unresponsive.

"I couldn't see a way out." Dilwyn let out a guttural groan, turning back to the DI. "I wish I hadn't gone out that night. If I could turn the clock back, believe me, I would. After we shot that lad, it was like we were stuck in a quicksand. And every move sucked us deeper. There seemed to be no way out. I'm glad of being arrested, if I'm honest."

Now was not the time to watch the man before her unravel, his wounded conscience wide open. Back at the station, they would book him and his son into custody and question them the following day, and take statements from Tony Jones and Keith Miller, the intended victims of that evening.

A part of her felt sorry for Dilwyn and Ryan. They were not hardened criminals, but neither were they simply ordinary men caught in terrible circumstances. Their behaviour had been deliberate in the concealment of a death and of a body. No wonder Keith, the career criminal, and his hardman friend Tony looked to be in shock. They would not have expected this.

"We will talk more tomorrow, Mr Jenkins," she said, signalling with her head for him to be taken away. "It's time for these officers to go home."

THE POLICE VAN'S heavy doors clanged shut, sealing the offenders in the cold metal cage in which they would feel every bump and turn as the vehicle made its way back to the station. They sat opposite each other, wrists handcuffed; separated by a space filled with regret.

The vehicle rumbled through the quiet streets of Newtown, its harsh suspension jarring the occupants at every pothole and speed bump.

Dilwyn's gaze fixed on the van's floor, tracing the scuff marks and dried mud left by countless others who had fallen foul of the law.

Outside, the world was a blur of shadows and streetlights. Some flickered like accusatory eyes, casting a strobed glare over the van and deserted pavements. Buildings stood silent in judgement as the van made its way to Park Lane.

Ryan stared blankly out of the window through the wire cage. Each reflection skidding across the glass was another reminder of the freedom they were about to lose. He swallowed hard "I'm sorry, Dad," he muttered, the words barely audible above the engine. "I'm sorry I took the gun up there that night. You didn't shoot him, I did. I got us both into this mess."

"We're in this together." Dilwyn tutted. "I'm never going to drink again. I can tell you that."

They fell into a doomed silence as the van approached the police station on Park Lane. Lights were on in the car park and some rooms above, but their destination was the bowels of the building and the large custody suite.

As the van pulled up, they saw the automatic doors of the building open, ready to receive them.

"End of the road," one officer declared, as he unlatched the door to let them out.

They stepped into a floodlit area, squinting as their eyes adjusted to the sudden brightness. They entered via a narrow room bathed in UV light.

"Move along," another officer directed, her tone betraying no emotion.

After the custody sergeant agreed the charges alleged by the arresting officers, the men were searched, and locked in the cells.

19

SMALL MERCIES

The early morning light coming through the briefing room windows highlighted faces etched with fatigue following the previous night's dramatic events.

DCI Chris Llewelyn sat at the head of the table, tie loose; sleeves rolled up. Yvonne could have sworn the grey streaks in his hair were more prominent. "Excellent work, again," he began, face serious. "Your quick thinking saved Tony Jones and Keith Miller from almost certain death or injury. We have put the community's minds at rest that we have Liam Stone's killer in custody, and have the explanation for why Ben, Tom, and Hayden died in the woods that night. Seriously well done."

Murmurs of acknowledgement rippled through the room, accompanied by a shuffle of papers and creak of chairs. Jones and Miller were far from saints, but the team's job was to protect without fear or favour, and that they had done.

"Yvonne," Llewelyn said, turning to the DI as the rest

team made their way back to the main office. He pressed his lips together. "I know you went into that situation before backup arrived." He sighed. "We've talked about this. I gave strict instruction to wait."

The light caught the white in her blonde hair, as her equally determined face met his gaze. "We heard Ryan Jones cock both barrels of his shotgun. He was ready to shoot. If I had waited, that gun would have gone off. I couldn't take that chance."

"But he already shot someone in exactly the same circumstances. You could have been the next Liam Stone."

"We announced who we were. I really felt it was the only way to prevent that gun from going off. Ryan Jenkins was about to fire. I don't see that I had any choice, sir."

He sighed. "I know your instincts were crucial last night. You read the situation right in the end, but I am not happy with the risks you take. I've told you before, you're one of the finest detectives I know. Your intuition is second-to-none. But I worry every time you are out there and that phone goes off." His eyes held hers. "You have been hospitalised more than once, and your vest cannot stop a shotgun blast at close range. I'm asking you, again, to be more careful, Yvonne. You narrowly avoided disciplinary eight months ago. Don't keep risking your life like that."

"Understood..." She nodded, her expression impassive. "And, by the way, it was Callum's quick thinking that alerted me to the potential situation in the park."

"He's an excellent officer." Llewelyn nodded. "He'll make a good DS one day."

"He will," she agreed.

~

Yvonne stoked the fire into a roaring blaze. Its amber glow sent shadows dancing around the walls as she listened to Tasha's tales of London and the case she had helped bring to a successful conclusion.

Dinner's remnants cleared away. They settled onto cushions spread over the rug, the heat from the fireplace warming them through as Tasha leaned back against the foot of the couch, yawning. "Home at last," she murmured, her words accompanied by the snap and hiss of fresh logs on the fire.

"I'm so glad you are home." Yvonne smiled. "You know, I think I hold my breath the entire time you are away."

The psychologist laughed. "I'm surprised you don't pass out."

The DI giggled. "I've been dreaming of some time away, just the two of us."

"You mean before our honeymoon?"

"Yes..."

"Where would you like to go?"

"What about France?" She sipped from her glass of chardonnay, eyes wistful.

"France?" Tasha cocked her head, another yawn escaping unbidden.

"Yes... I know we said later in the year for our honeymoon, but the London case concluded sooner than you expected. Perhaps, before my next big case comes along, we could have a week away. Somewhere romantic; steeped in history. What do you say?"

"I could quite fancy France," the psychologist nodded, her eyes on the fire. "What about Le Puy?"

"Le Puy?" Yvonne reached for her laptop.

Tasha nodded. "I went there once during a conference. I

didn't get the chance to explore properly, but what I saw from the train and bus looked fascinating. Castle ruins and chapels perched on giant volcanic plugs. Not too busy, but plenty to see, it seemed."

The DI stretched her legs, the laptop resting on top. "Le Puy, I've never been there," she said, fingers tapping keys. "Okay, I have it. Le Puy en Velay." She read from aloud from a travel blog, in an exaggerated French accent. "I like the sound of that name." She continued reading. "Nestled in the Auvergne, in the heart of France, the city of Le Puy is a tapestry of cobblestone streets winding through ancient architecture. Volcanic crags rise like sentinels around the town, crowned with monuments that have stood watch over the city for centuries. Wow... It sounds intriguing." She sighed, relaxing back against the cushions. "The spire of Saint-Michel d'Aiguilhe pierces the heavens atop its rocky pinnacle, while Notre-Dame de France surveys the landscape with serene grace."

"Let's book it." Tasha reached for her hand. "I can see us wandering those cobblestone streets, hunting down French cuisine, and shouting from atop those crags."

"I'll book it in the morning." Yvonne put down her laptop and wine glass. "I think you and I could both do with the break. Would you like a hot chocolate before bed?"

"I'd love that." The psychologist glanced at the clock. It was nine-thirty.

Ten minutes later, the DI was back from the kitchen with two steaming, chunky mugs. She paused, in two minds whether to disturb her partner whose eyes were now closed. Deciding to sit next to her instead, she placed the second mug down on the rug and leaned her head on Tasha's shoulder, simply glad to have her wife back safe from her London sojourn.

Sighing with contentment as the fire caressed her face, she sipped from her mug of chocolate and held her hand next to Tasha's, comparing their rings. She smiled. This felt right. It felt like home.

THE END.

AFTERWORD

Coming soon:
Watch out for Book 3 in the DI McKenzie Series and Book 23 in the DI Giles Series.

Mailing list: You can join my emailing list here : AnnamarieMorgan.com
Facebook page: AnnamarieMorganAuthor

You might also like to read the other books in the DI Giles Series:

Book 1: Death Master:
After months of mental and physical therapy, Yvonne Giles, an Oxford DI, is back at work and that's just how she likes it. So when she's asked to hunt the serial killer responsible for taking apart young women, the DI jumps at the chance but hides the fact she is suffering debilitating flashbacks. She is told to work with Tasha Phillips, an in-her-face, criminal psychologist. The DI is not enamoured with the idea. Tasha has a lot to prove. Yvonne has a lot to get

over. A tentative link with a 20 year-old cold case brings them closer to the truth but events then take a horrifyingly personal turn.

Book 2: You Will Die

After apprehending an Oxford Serial Killer, and almost losing her life in the process, DI Yvonne Giles has left England for a quieter life in rural Wales.Her peace is shattered when she is asked to hunt a priest-killing psychopath, who taunts the police with messages inscribed on the corpses.Yvonne requests the help of Dr. Tasha Phillips, a psychologist and friend, to aid in the hunt. But the killer is one step ahead and the ultimatum, he sets them, could leave everyone devastated.

Book 3: Total Wipeout

A whole family is wiped out with a shotgun. At first glance, it's an open-and-shut case. The dad did it, then killed himself. The deaths follow at least two similar family wipeouts – attributed to the financial crash.

So why doesn't that sit right with Detective Inspector Yvonne Giles? And why has a rape occurred in the area, in the weeks preceding each family's demise? Her seniors do not believe there are questions to answer. DI Giles must therefore risk everything, in a high-stakes investigation ofa mysterious masonic ring and players in high finance.

Can she find the answers, before the next innocent family is wiped out?

Book 4: Deep Cut

In a tiny hamlet in North Wales, a female recruit is murdered whilst on Christmas home leave. Detective Inspector Yvonne Giles is asked to cut short her own leave, to investigate. Why was the young soldier killed? And is her death related to several alleged suicides at her army base? DI Giles this it is, and that someone powerful has a dark secret they will do anything to hide.

Book 5: The Pusher

Young men are turning up dead on the banks of the River Severn. Some of them have been missing for days or even weeks. The only thing the police can be sure of, is that the men have drowned. Rumours abound that a mythical serial killer has turned his attention from the Manchester canal to the waterways of Mid-Wales. And now one of CID's own is missing. A brand new recruit with everything to live for. DI Giles must find him before it's too late.

Book 6: Gone

Children are going missing. They are not heard from again until sinister requests for cryptocurrency go viral. The public must pay or the children die. For lead detective Yvonne Giles, the case is complicated enough. And then the unthinkable happens...

Book 7: Bone Dancer

A serial killer is murdering women, threading their bones back together, and leaving them for police to find. Detective Inspector Yvonne Giles must find him before more innocent victims die. Problem is, the killer wants her and will do anything he can to get her. Unaware that she, herself, is is a target, DI Giles risks everything to catch him.

Book 8: Blood Lost

A young man comes home to find his whole family missing. Half-eaten breakfasts and blood spatter on the lounge wall are the only clues to what happened...

Book 9: Angel of Death

The peace of the Mid-Wales countryside is shattered, when a female eco-warrior is found crucified in a public wood. At first, it would appear a simple case of finding which of the woman's enemies had had her killed. But DI Yvonne Giles has no idea how bad things are going to get. As the body count rises, she will need all of her instincts, and the skills of those closest to her, to stop the murderous rampage of the Angel of Death.

Book 10: Death in the Air

Several fatal air collisions have occurred within a few months in rural Wales. According to the local Air Accidents Investigation Branch (AAIB) inspector, it's a coincidence. Clusters happen. Except, this cluster is different. DI Yvonne Giles suspects it when she hears some of the witness statements but, when an AAIB inspector is found dead under a bridge, she knows it.

Something is way off. Yvonne is determined to get to the bottom of the mystery, but exactly how far down the treacherous rabbit hole is she prepared to go?

Book 11: Death in the Mist

The morning after a viscous sea-mist covers the seaside town of Aberystwyth, a young student lies brutalised within one hundred yards of the castle ruins.

DI Yvonne Giles' reputation precedes her. Having successfully captured more serial killers than some detectives have caught colds, she is seconded to head the murder investigation team, and hunt down the young woman's killer.

What she doesn't know, is this is only the beginning...

Book 12: Death under Hypnosis

When the secretive and mysterious Sheila Winters approaches Yvonne Giles and tells her that she murdered someone thirty years before, she has the DI's immediate attention.

Things get even more strange when Sheila states:

She doesn't know who.

She doesn't know where.

She doesn't know why.

Book 13: Fatal Turn

A seasoned hiker goes missing from the Dolfor Moors after recording a social media video describing a narrow cave he intends to explore. A tragic accident? Nothing to see here, until a team of cavers disappear on a coastal potholing expedition, setting off a string of events that has DI Giles tearing her hair out. What, or who is the thread that ties this series of disappearances together?

A serial killer, thriller murder-mystery set in Wales.

Book 14: The Edinburgh Murders

A newly-retired detective from the Met is murdered in a murky alley in Edinburgh, a sinister calling card left with the body.

The dead man had been a close friend of psychologist Tasha Phillips, giving her her first gig with the Met decades before.

Tasha begs DI Yvonne Giles to aid the Scottish police in solving the case.

In unfamiliar territory, and with a ruthless killer haunting the streets, the DI plunges herself into one of the darkest, most terrifying cases of her career. Who exactly is The Poet?

Book 15: A Picture of Murder

Men are being thrown to their deaths in rural Wales.

At first glance, the murders appear unconnected until DI Giles uncovers potential links with a cold case from the turn of the Millennium.

Someone is eliminating the witnesses to a double murder.

DI Giles and her team must find the perpetrator before all the witnesses are dead.

Book 16: The Wilderness Murders

People are disappearing from remote locations.

Abandoned cars, neatly piled belongings, and bizarre last photographs, are the only clues for what happened to them.

Did they run away? Or, as DI Giles suspects, have they fallen prey to a serial killer who is taunting police with the heinous pieces of a puzzle they must solve if they are to stop the wilderness murderer.

Book 17: The Bunker Murders

A murder victim found in a shallow grave has DI Yvonne Giles and her team on the hunt for both the killer and a motive for the well-loved man's demise.

Yvonne cannot help feeling the killing is linked to a string of female disappearances stretching back nearly two decades.

Someone has all the answers, and the DI will stop at

nothing to find them and get to the bottom of this perplexing mystery.

Book 18: The Garthmyl Murders

A missing brother and friends with dark secrets have DI Giles turning circles after a body is found face-down in the pond of a local landmark.

Stymied by a wall of silence and superstition, Yvonne and her team must dig deeper than ever if they are to crack this impossible case.

Who, or what, is responsible for the Garthmyl murders?

Book 19: The Signature

When a young woman is found dead inside a rubbish dumpster after a night out, police chiefs are quick to label it a tragic accident. But as more bodies surface, Detective Inspector Yvonne Giles is convinced a cold-blooded murderer is on the loose. She believes the perpetrator is devious and elusive, disabling CCTV cameras in the area, and leaving them with little to go on. With time running out, Giles and her team must race against the clock to catch the killer or killers before they strike again.

Book 20: The Incendiary Murders

When the Powys mansion belonging to an ageing rock star is rocked by a deadly explosion, Detective Inspector Yvonne Giles finds herself tasked with a case of murder, suspicion, and secrets. As shockwaves ripple through the community, Giles must pierce the impenetrable facades of the characters surrounding the case, racing the clock to find the culprit and prevent further bombings. With an investigation full of twists and turns, DI Yvonne Giles must unravel the truth before it's too late.

Book 21 - The Park Murders

When two people are left dead and four others are seriously ill in hospital after a visit to a local nature park in rural Wales, DI Giles and her team find themselves in a race against time to stop a killer or killers hell-bent on terrorising the community. As the investigation deepens, the team must draw on all of their skill and experience to hunt down the elusive Powys poisoner before more lives are lost.

Book 22 - The Powys Murders

Three bodies are discovered in a wood when snow and ice melt from the Powys countryside. Police suspect the dead men were involved in a road traffic collision before they ran off into the darkness and succumbed to exposure.

What made them run uphill into the wilderness instead of downhill to the nearest town? Were all of their injuries inflicted by the collision? Or something more sinister? And why was one victim missing his shoes?

DI Yvonne Giles suspects foul play, believing the men ran the wrong way because they were terrified. Who, or what, was responsible for the deaths of The Powys Three? And are others at risk from the same evil?

Remember to watch out for Book 3 in the DI McKenzie Series, coming soon...

Printed in Great Britain
by Amazon